Ne'faro

THE INVASION

Roxane, Please accept
this gift, courtesy of
Karla.

Jeffrey

04/13/2021

JEFFREY OGBONNAYA

NEWMAN SPRINGS PUBLISHING
320 Broad Street
Red Bank, NJ 07701

First originally published by Newman Springs Publishing 2020

ISBN 978-1-64531-850-7 (Paperback)
ISBN 978-1-64801-484-0 (Hardcover)
ISBN 978-1-64531-851-4 (Digital)

Printed in the United States of America

To Dolly

CHAPTER 1

Don't Blame Me—I Was Curious!

Max and Damian squirmed and wailed as a bright-blue-colored liquid streamed into the tubes they were trapped in. A woman dressed in a white lab coat stood by and watched. Time seemed to slow as they struggled to recall the events of the day and how they ended up in captivity.

It had been a rather uneventful day for them. They went through their regular morning routines and went off to school in their solar-powered school bus. School went on as usual except for a boring science lesson they'd had about climate change. Their fourth grade teacher taught them that sixty-four years prior, world leaders, after many years of disagreement, came to terms with the reality of global warming and joined their hands to combat it. Laws, policies, and standards were put in place to limit the use of fossil fuels and cut down carbon emission. That's how the Earth was spared a major extinction event. But hey, it was easy enough that they didn't get homework on it.

With no homework and lots of time on their hands, they decided to race each other to a local arcade after school. Damian was leading and took a different route than they usually did. Max followed him and, three blocks down the new street, spotted a tall and majestic building with a holographic signage that read "Universal Labs."

"That's cool," Max said. "Let's go inside!"

"Yeah, it's cool, but when has common sense told you to go inside random buildings?" Damian asked.

Max didn't answer.

"Oh! Never," Damian remarked, nevertheless following his friend.

Max grunted, walking up to the door. It slid open, allowing them entry.

They walked inside and were greeted by another holographic sign that said "Welcome to Universal Labs!" It was an open space bounded by pearly-white walls at the far ends. A number of visitors were seated on plush upholstered chairs that decorated the lobby and made it look more like a five-star hotel lounge. Transparent glass partitions allowed them to view a more extensive space dotted with a variety of colors from chemical mixtures in assorted flasks, beakers, and tubes. They could also see the hustle and bustle of workers doing their various jobs.

"Wait," Damian said. "How big *is* this place?"

"However big the people who created the space wanted it to be," Max responded.

Before they could converse any more, a lady in a white lab coat walked up to them. "Do you need anything?" she asked the boys.

"Not necessarily, but now that I'm thinking about it, maybe an interactive tour of this place?" Max answered.

The woman stroked her chin. "Well, for safety reasons, I'm afraid I can't allow you boys to have a hands-on experience here. But I can certainly give you a tour and explain things as we go, if that's okay with you."

"That's all right," Damian said, letting his guard down. Max nodded in agreement, savoring the kindness of the woman.

The woman led them to a locked door just to the left of the glass partitions. She gazed at the door for a moment, and a pulsating red light flashed for two seconds, followed by a clicking sound. The door gently swung open for them, and they stepped into a small room with another door to their right. The same process was repeated, and the door opened, letting them out into a long hallway. As they walked down, the woman explained what went on behind each of the doors that lined the hallway.

"That's where we figure out properties of new chemicals," she said when they came to one room. And with another, she said, "This is the zero-grav room, where we play around with gravity and study its effects." At the end of the hallway, she motioned to the boys. "We will take the flight of stairs."

"Can we please go in the elevators?" Max asked.

"Not a chance," she responded. "Those hover elevators are too fast for my liking. And besides, I'm claustrophobic."

Max and Damian followed her up the stairs and into another hallway. They couldn't help but be amazed at the sheer size of the building and what went on in each space. But then, after what seemed like forever, they stepped into a large room with no windows. Right in front of them were four large transparent tubes with open walk-in doors.

"What are those?" Damian asked, surveying the room.

"We experiment with hurricane-force winds here. Someone steps inside, shutting the door behind them, and we set the winds in motion with this control pad," the woman explained, pointing at a four-foot-tall cylindrical mount with a rectangular touch screen on top. "It's lots of fun. Why don't you two try it?" she suggested, shutting the door to the room behind them.

"Umm, why don't we—"

Damian was cut off by the woman, who, in one swift move, shoved him into the rightmost tube and Max in the left. She secured the door latches and said, grinning evilly, "Let's get down to business." She walked back to the control pad and touched a blue button, which triggered the flow of the bright-blue-colored liquid.

* * * * *

Meanwhile, a battle was raging on Venta-16. The Ne'faro, an evil race of aliens from Ne'far, had taken the planet by storm. They had light-blue skin and were uniformly dressed in shiny silver armor made of a very hard crystal that gave them utmost protection. And they were just as adept in battle as any other race.

Warriors from many different planets had gathered to ward off the group of Ne'faro. Each squad of warriors from the various planets possessed a unique Warrior Energy characteristic of their place of origin and were led by a commander. Their weapons and armor allowed them to take down enemies without taking much damage.

Commander Crogan from Glacies-9 and Commander Ragnar from Ignis were fighting back to back. They were fierce and perfectly synchronized. Ragnar wore an armor made from Ignisean obsidian. This obsidian was many times more protective than any material known to man and was also fireproof. It was for this reason that Ragnar had his armor coated with fire. He held a sharp five-foot-long fiery chain that burned and cut on contact, making Ragnar a force to be reckoned with. Crogan wore a special ice armor that was equally protective. He wielded a three-foot-long sword that froze anything it touched.

The two were almost an unstoppable force. *Almost.* They had pushed back most of their Ne'faro attackers, but they kept regrouping.

"A hundred fifty to two? I like our odds," Ragnar said sarcastically.

The two commanders were so caught up fighting, though, that they didn't notice themselves slowly spreading apart. They also didn't notice the Ne'faro soldier creeping in between them.

Just as they were about to cut down more enemies, two lethally poisoned daggers flashed. The soldier thrust them simultaneously at the two commanders, and they stopped in midair. They fell to the ground. In one last move, they decided to carry their Warrior Energies to other people who could continue their legacy. They touched their swords together, and a ball of light pulsed, pushing the Ne'faro back. The two commanders collapsed on the ground, dead, and their energies flew off toward Earth.

* * * * *

Back in the tubes, Max and Damian were standing on their toes, just to keep their nostrils above fluid level a little longer. They pounded on the tubes, but both knew they couldn't escape. The woman tapped on her ear pods, saying, "The experiment is going as planned. Our two new subjects are resisting, but they won't be escaping on my watch."

The boys looked up right as bright lights flashed above their heads, and there was a moment of stillness. Above Damian's head shone a blue light, and above Max's head shone an orange one.

Suddenly there was a loud explosion. The tubes blasted open with a rush of air, and the boys fell out.

Max looked at Damian and realized that he was frozen in an exact ice sculpture of himself and wasn't moving. Max groaned, ran at the ice, and punched it. It left a red mark that quickly grew brighter, melted the ice, and started a fire.

While flames licked at him, Damian, springing onto his feet, shouted at Max, "See? I told you we shouldn't go into this building."

"Don't blame me, I was curious!" Max retorted. "And by the way, we've just gotten some special powers," he added.

After rolling his eyes, Damian launched himself off the ground. He flipped over the woman while Max slid under her legs, both successfully escaping their captor into the hallway.

The boys ran as fast as they could and jumped out the window at the end of the hallway. While midair, Damian created an ice slide, and they slid all the way down. The wind whipped through their hair as they made their way down. Max got down last and shot a fireball to melt the slide.

"Look!" Damian yelled, and Max turned around to see a squad of police floating toward them in hover cars. Apparently, the explosion had startled the city and attracted the police. People were also beginning to crowd around Universal Labs but away from the police.

The police positioned their laser rifles and aimed. One officer screamed into his megaphone, "Hands up!"

Max put his hands in the air, and flames gathered in them. *Rats*, he thought, realizing his hands were on fire.

"He's a threat. Fire!"

They fired at Max. Damian focused and created an ice shield that blocked the lasers while Max threw fireballs and destroyed their hover cars.

* * * * *

Sprinting toward the scene were Ashleigh and Jessica, two of Damian and Max's classmates. They were on their way to the water park after school for a play date when the explosion happened. It had shaken the ground lightly, and smoke was billowing out of the roof of Universal Labs. The girls noticed it and ran in the direction of the smoke, wanting to know what had transpired there. A few blocks to Universal Labs, the girls stopped, panting.

"Can't breathe!" Ashleigh wheezed, bending over.

"And my leg muscles are sore," Jessica responded. Placing her hand on Ashleigh's back, she tapped her gently and as if in rhythm with her own breathing.

Then a shimmering mist appeared above Jessica's head, and a bright white light shone above Ashleigh's. Jessica noticed them right away as they pulsed and disappeared. Instantly, the girls felt relief from their aching muscles and shortness of breath.

"How did we recover that fast?" Ashleigh asked, eyeing herself.

"Maybe it had something to do with those glowy things that appeared above our heads," Jessica replied.

"What glowy things?" Ashleigh asked.

"They appeared right after you said you couldn't breathe," Jessica explained.

Ashleigh played with her hair with her index fingers. "So they must have had something to do with that," she deduced.

"I guess," Jessica agreed. They then picked themselves off the ground and dusted themselves off, resuming their sprint. The girls' speed was doubled, and they soon reached Universal Labs.

The first thing they noticed was the huge crowd. The second thing they noticed was the police. They also noticed firefighters battling the huge fire on the east side of the Universal Labs building.

The final thing they noticed was two of their classmates being fired at by the police.

"Is that Max?" Ashleigh asked.

"And Damian?" Jessica added.

Ashleigh waved her hands at the police, yelling at them to stop firing. But out of the blue, a bolt of lightning flew from her hand and struck a police vehicle.

"What?" Ashleigh yelled in disbelief. "How did that happen?"

Jessica had already analyzed the situation. "I think this might be part of what the light did to you." But it didn't matter. The police force had spotted them. "Run!" Jessica said. "Go toward Max and Damian."

The two dashed toward the boys, joining them. Max gave them a quick glance, turning back to the police. Max shot warning flames, and Ashleigh created a ball filled with electricity. The police fired, and Damian quickly created an ice shield that deflected the lasers. Jessica raised her right hand into the air, closing her eyes. A stream of water swirled around her hand. She formed it into a ball, throwing it at a hover car. It exploded, and Max used the fire from the vehicle to set another hover car on fire. Then police hover cars started firing laser missiles, but Damian deflected them with his handy-dandy shields.

Max threw fireballs at the police, keeping their attention on him. Meanwhile, Ashleigh and Jessica ran straight at the cars and used their powers to destroy them while Damian protected them with ice. Damian created ice daggers while protecting himself with a shield. He launched the daggers, and Ashleigh boosted them with electricity to help them hit their targets: the cars. The blades whizzed through the air toward the cars, and they flew true. The moment they impacted the hover cars, they exploded.

Max shot weak flames that hit a few police and made their clothing catch fire, making them fall over screaming. Besides that, though, the police just used more lasers to try and hit them. They missed every single one of them.

Max rubbed his hands together, and a spiral of fire grew around his hands. He threw it, and it exploded on the police force, sending them flying through the air and dropping them into the water-park pools. Ashleigh and Max cheered and went over to Jessica and Damian. They all walked to Max's house while calling their parents on their smart earbuds to give them the address.

When they arrived at Max's house, Max walked onto the front porch and rang the doorbell. The door unlocked, and Max's mom's face peeked out. "Max!" she said, hugging her son.

"Hey, Mom," Max said, smiling.

"You brought friends too!" Max's mother squealed.

"I brought something else," Max said, lighting his hand on fire.

"How did you do that?" Max's mom asked, taking a step back.

"I'll explain inside," Max said, walking in and extinguishing his fire.

The four kids walked into Max's house. Max removed his sneakers and set them on a shoe rack. He gestured to his friends to do the same. Once they had all removed their shoes, they sat down on Max's long blue shapeshifting couch. With a click of a button on the armrest, the couch could change from a couch to a bed and more. Sometimes if they were tired enough, Max and his mom would change the couch to bed form and sleep. That setting was very convenient.

Ashleigh grabbed a furry pillow off the couch and melted into it, loving its soft feel.

"Oh, Mom?" Max said, turning toward his mother.

"Yes?" Max's mom answered.

"Is it okay if my friends' parents come too?" Max asked, crossing his fingers.

"Sure!" Max's mother replied, beaming. "The more, the merrier. Let me get some snacks prepared for all of us."

"Can I help, Mrs. Channing?" Ashleigh asked.

"Sure. And please call me Amy," Max's mom answered.

Ashleigh lifted herself off the couch and walked with Amy to the kitchen. Jessica leaned over to Max. "Did you ever tell Ashleigh your last name?" she asked.

Max frowned. "She probably learned it on the first day of school when we all had to introduce ourselves with our first and last names."

"Okay," Jessica said.

Suddenly the doorbell rang, and Max got up to get it. *It's probably Damian's, Ashleigh's, and Jessica's parents*, he thought. He opened the door, and sure enough, their parents were standing outside. "Come in," Max said, gesturing to another shape-shifting recliner couch. This one was orange.

Only four adults could fit on that couch, so the remaining two spilled over onto the blue one with the kids. "Lemme go check with my mom. Be right back," Max said, walking into the kitchen.

Amy and Ashleigh were busy making Amy's reputable cookie sandwiches with vanilla cookies and chocolate. "That looks good!" Max commented, smiling at the two females.

Max sniffed the air, and sure enough, the unique scent of vanilla and chocolate caught his attention. Then Max walked around the two ladies and saw the full extent of the cookie-sandwich making. There were well over a dozen cookie sandwiches on a tray, and Ashleigh and Amy were working hard to double the number.

"Let me help," Max said, washing his hands with water from the kitchen sink.

Max took two cookies and grabbed another butter knife, dipping it in their jar of Nutella. He spread the chocolate on the flat end of a round wafer-like cookie. He then put another cookie on top of the chocolate side, creating one cookie sandwich. He repeated this process dozens more times, greatly contributing to the number of cookies.

In about five minutes, the three had made over six dozen cookie sandwiches, all of them fitting on two trays. "Whew! That was fun but tiring," Ashleigh remarked, grabbing a tray and carrying it to the living room.

Amy smiled in agreement, grabbing another tray and following Ashleigh. The two set the trays down on a hovering table, and everyone turned to it. "What are those?" Jessica asked.

"They're Amy's famous cookie sandwiches! Those things are delicious, trust me!" Damian said excitedly.

Amy laughed, gesturing toward the trays. "Please, everyone, have some."

Damian and Jessica glanced at each other, grinning. They grabbed lots of cookie sandwiches, scarfing them down. Even the adults seemed to like them, taking one whenever they'd get the chance.

"So," Amy started, looking at Max, "how'd you get the ability to create fire?"

Max shrugged. "I guess it was the bright light that appeared above my head while we were trapped in Universal Labs."

"And by *we* you mean…?" Amy asked her son.

"By that I mean me and Damian," Max said.

Everyone except the kids gasped.

"So Damian has this power too?" Damian's father asked.

Max shook his head. "He doesn't have fire manipulation, but rather…," he trailed off, gesturing to Damian.

Damian raised his right hand into the air, and ice and snow swirled around it. The room temperature dropped by twenty degrees. "Ice," Damian finished. He dropped his hand, and the temperature increased to its normal.

"Now that that cat's out of the bag, let us girls show you ours," Ashleigh said. Electricity crackled in her hands, and the air became filled with static charge. Jessica created a stream of water and made it twist and curl in the air, much to everyone's appeal.

But Amy's eyebrows narrowed. "You said you boys were trapped in Universal Labs?"

"Yes," Max said. "We were led to a large room with two tubes by a lady in a white lab coat. She tried to drown us with this blue liquid. But then we got our powers, and the tubes exploded. Damian was frozen in ice, so I punched it, not knowing that my punch would make the ice explode. That explosion melted the ice and started a fire. Damian and I then escaped through a window down the passageway, getting down on a slide made of ice, courtesy of Damian. Then we were attacked by the police, but the girls came to our aid and helped us fend off the large force. And from there, we walked to here, this house."

This was a lot of information for the adults in the room, but they responded with "I see" or "Okay." After more questions like "Are you hurt?" the families went their separate ways, but not before Amy exchanged contacts with all the other parents. Max had a sneaky suspicion this wouldn't be the last time his mom would see his friends' parents.

After saying all their goodbyes, the other families left, and Max ran up to his room to practice on his powers. He became so engrossed that, that night, he only got six hours of sleep.

CHAPTER 2

This Is an Alien Invasion, Please Remain Calm

It was the last day of school. Max and Ashleigh had missed the bus and had no other option than to travel the one and a half miles by foot. At the same time, Ashleigh was trying very hard to create a hoverboard out of electricity. She held her hands out in front of her and willed the electricity to form a hoverboard. But her powers had been unwilling to work, so she was having quite a hard time.

Then Max noticed and said, "Close your eyes and imagine the shape of the object you're trying to make. Imagine where it would be on the ground and what color it would be. Then open your eyes and channel your energy toward that spot, still imagining the construct."

Ashleigh nodded, stopping abruptly. She looked at the ground, memorizing its details. Then she closed her eyes and imagined a yellow electric hoverboard with sparks flying from it. She opened her eyes and channeled her energy, electric sparks shooting off the ground. Finally, a yellow sparking hoverboard formed, and Ashleigh mounted it.

From that point on, she was always at least six feet in front of Max—that is, until he finally got tired of it. With a flick of his wrist, fiery tendrils erupted from the ground, wrapped around Ashleigh's ankles, and lifted her into the air. She squealed and started kicking and flailing her legs until Max set her down.

Ashleigh pouted. "How are you so good?"

"Practice makes perfect," Max said casually. He then added, "I perfected the fiery-tendril thing last night, making sure it doesn't set things on fire. Unless I want to, of course." Fiery roller skates appeared in place of his sneakers. "Race you to school!" he called, wheeling away.

"Oh no, you don't!" Ashleigh yelled. Her hoverboard reappeared, this time with two jets on either side. She shot off after Max, her hair flying with the wind.

Max blazed across the sidewalk and glanced back at Ashleigh. He noticed she was gaining on him, but he didn't notice the jets on either side of her skateboard. With a single thought, the jets activated and boosted Ashleigh ahead of Max. Instead of the surprised look she *imagined* he'd have, he grinned, and his hands lit on fire.

Two fireballs took out the jets on the hoverboard, and it started to slow down. Max held one arm out and faced his palm toward her. A single dot of fire appeared in the middle of his palm, and eight more appeared around it. Then they all started spinning violently. All of a sudden, nine fiery tendrils erupted out of the ground and swarmed Ashleigh, pinning her down. Ashleigh struggled against the warm orange restraints, but they were too strong, and there were too many of them. *Darn*, Ashleigh thought.

Max's roller skates disappeared, and he smirked, a fireball in his hand. "Looks like I win," he said triumphantly.

Ashleigh closed her eyes and pictured a clone of herself appearing behind Max. A voice sounded behind him, "Not if I have anything to say about it!" There was a yellow and white flash, and Max fell to his knees. The fire cage disappeared, and Ashleigh walked out, high-fiving her clone before she dissipated into tiny electrons.

Suddenly a tall man tackled Max! They went down hard and rolled across the road until they hit a building. Max got to his feet, backing up. Ashleigh sprinted after them, summoning lightning. The air went dry. The man smiled unconvincingly and kicked Max's leg. Just as he sprung off the ground, a lightning bolt struck his chest, sending him sprawling. Max rolled onto his feet and flicked his wrist. Flaming tendrils wrapped around the man's ankles and sent him into the air. He struggled, then stopped. He looked directly at Max while he rolled his eyes continuously, and they started spiraling. Max tried to look away, but it was too late. His own eyes crossed, and his fists lit on fire. But instead of their regular orange color, they were a dark purple. Max slowly turned to Ashleigh, and she charged.

"Woah," Max started, "let's talk about this like civilized, non-super-powered preteens."

Ashleigh glanced at his hands. "Yeah, let's talk while your hands are on fire. *That's* totally normal."

"Come on, join me and Sam," Max coaxed.

Sam? Ashleigh thought. "I'd rather have a permanent Lichtenberg scar!" she said to Max.

"What a shame. Guess I have to destroy you now." Max sighed. He rushed Ashleigh, and she barely stepped out of the way. She imagined her hoverboard appearing on the ground in front of her and channeled her energy into it. The jet-powered hoverboard materialized with a crackling sound, and Ashleigh jumped onto it, powering it up instantly. Max regained his bearings and ran after her, his roller skates forming. He was close behind her, slowly gaining. A fireball flew at Ashleigh, and she ducked, narrowly avoiding losing any hairs. A light pole was coming into view, and Max was getting even closer.

Ashleigh, adrenaline making her brain work faster, slowed down and allowed Max to get really close to her. Max was now only one foot behind Ashleigh, but it was exactly what she wanted. *He'll never see this one coming*, Ashleigh thought.

Then the moment the light pole was within her reach, Ashleigh lightly moved to the right and grabbed it. She twisted her body around it and thundered in the left direction perpendicular to Max's. What happened to Max? You could say his "you may kiss the bride" moment came a little earlier than expected.

Ashleigh turned around the corner of the street and came into the school's parking lot. Grinning to herself, she left her tiny hoverboard in the middle of a parking space and ran into the school building.

She wove through the white-floored halls packed with kids, aiming for her classroom. "C'mon," she whispered to herself. She turned right through the hallway, spotting the classroom she needed. She sprinted down the hallway and entered the room.

"Damian. Jessica," she hissed, panting. "Follow me."

Luckily, the teacher was out of the room, and they hurried out.

"What's wrong?" Jessica asked.

"It's Ma—"

An explosion broke the wall in front of them into tiny pieces of dust, and Max appeared, his face red.

"—x," Ashleigh finished.

"Pathetic, pathetic." Max sneered.

"Did you *really* think you could hide?" He threw a fireball. Damian created a shield in front of Ashleigh but fell to the ground when the fireball melted it and hit him. Max threw another fireball at Ashleigh. She put two fingers in front of her nose and did a backflip over the fireball, throwing a long chain of lightning at him.

Max slapped it away and charged at her. An icy wind swirled around Damian, and the ground frosted over. Max slipped and fell flat on his stomach. Damian raised his arms, and the ice raised, slamming Max into the ceiling. Ashleigh thought he was finished. That is, until the ice exploded, and Max hovered down. He dragged Damian by the arm, threw him up into the air, flew up above him, and shot a fire beam. Damian fell from the air, and it was at that moment that Ashleigh noticed the students crowded around them.

"Run!" Ashleigh yelled to the kids as Max turned toward them. The mob ran out of the building, screaming, "We're all going to die!"

"Water fountain me!" Jessica yelled, a ball of water forming in her hands. Ashleigh threw a bolt of lightning at an electric water fountain, and it fritzed, spraying water everywhere. Jessica spun all that water into a whirlpool and held it there. Max had already finished creating his own fireball. The two thrust their attacks at each other.

The opposing elements of fire and water merged with a powerful burst of air, creating a thick fog-like steam.

Now that I remember, a small shock to the brain could render him unconscious, Ashleigh thought. *If it goes bad, there's always the hospital.*

Ashleigh took the chance and ran quickly toward Max, shrouded by the steam. She got behind him and held an electric spark between her index and middle fingers. She placed her fingers on either side of his head and then the top. He collapsed on the ground in front of her.

The steam spun into a small cloud, courtesy of Jessica's water manipulation. All was calm, but if you've ever read books like this before, then you'll know that all is *never* well. Max stirred and lifted his head off the ground. Damian got to his feet and jumped into a crouched battle position, snow and ice swirling around his hands. Then Max brought himself to a sitting position, rubbing his head.

"Oww," he muttered.

Damian ran over to Max, helping him up. Ashleigh pumped her fist into the air, and Jessica snickered. "Crush, much?" Jessica whispered.

Ashleigh's face flushed. "Keep dreaming," she said, convincing nobody.

Damian and Jessica walked up to the broken wall. Jessica surrounded the rubble with water and lifted them up, arranging them into the hole in the wall.

"Boy, am I glad the three of us worked together to defeat Max. He would've blitzed us if we took him one by one!" Damian said, sealing the wall with ice.

Max stared straight at his feet and narrowed his eyes. He seemed to wobble at first, but slowly rose into the air. Damian stared in envy.

"He learned how to hover. My life is over!"

Max hovered to an exit at the end of the hall and opened the door. The group rushed after him and came out into the parking lot. "Freedom!" Ashleigh said joyfully. "We saved—"

A sudden movement to her right caught her attention. Hundreds, thousands, of weird-looking beings were on the roof, surrounding the school, and on the streets.

"This is an alien invasion. Please remain calm," Sam yelled from behind them.

"It's an ambush," Max whispered. "I was the distraction while that dude turned the entire city into an aliens' town." He then dropped to his feet. There was a moment of silence. Then the cries of the aliens echoed around the kids, and they charged.

"Don't hurt them!" Ashleigh screamed. "They're innocent civilians."

"Yeah," Damian said, throwing an alien off his back, "real innocent."

Max threw a fireball at another alien.

"Guys, there's a better way. Remember that thing I did to Max that broke the mind control on him?" Ashleigh asked.

Jessica nodded. "Yeah."

"Well, I could do it again. Keep them restrained, and I'll work my magic," Ashleigh continued.

"Oh!" They all nodded, catching on.

Max tapped his foot on the ground. Dozens of fiery tendrils wrapped themselves around the aliens' legs. Jessica tied a water chain around an alien's arms and stepped back. The water chain extended itself onto another alien's arm, then another. It spread across the horde faster than the plague.

Ashleigh's fingers sparked with electric charge as she flew across the chain of aliens. Every time she touched an alien, their head would droop; then a spark would link them to another alien. When Ashleigh finished with all of them, her hands glowed bright yellow. She clenched her fists, and the aliens screamed in pain, their shouts becoming more and more human.

Without warning, Sam appeared behind Ashleigh. Max and Damian looked at each other, then nodded. Max punched the guy in the arm, leaving a glowing red mark. The mark exploded and sent the guy flying right into Damian's ice beam. He froze, and Damian set him down in front of Max. Max added a bit of fire, and the two worked together to raise it.

They spun it around, gaining momentum, and chucked it as far as they could. Someone would probably find it later, but for now, it got the job done.

Sam's grip on the civilians had finally loosened, and they were shuffling around, trying to get back to wherever they were before Sam abducted them.

All in a good day's work, Ashleigh thought.

"Who wants pizza? I'm hungry," Max said.

They all agreed.

"Maybe Pizza Hut," Ashleigh suggested.

"Domino's bought that," Max said, leading them to the nearest Domino's pizza place.

CHAPTER 3

Emo Kid Destroys Half the City!

The kids walked into the building, and Max walked up to the counter.

"How may I help you?" asked the cashier. Max glanced at the menu on the wall in front of him, studying its contents.

"I'll have a large beef pizza, please. And four medium-sized drink cups. We'll take care of the drinks."

The cashier nodded, typing out the order. "That'll be thirty dollars, fifty cents."

"All right," Max said. He looked at the payment screen at the counter, and it scanned his face. His digital wallet appeared on the screen, and Max selected his crypto account to make his payment. It then scanned his fingerprint, and a green check mark appeared, securing the payment. The cashier then left to go get the food.

Max walked back to his friends, gesturing toward an open table. They sat down at the table, waiting for their food to be served. A waiter placed four plastic cups on their table, and each of the kids grabbed one, getting up. They all spotted the drink dispenser, dashing toward it.

Max filled his cup with pineapple-flavored soda, the others filling theirs with either cherry or grape. They walked back to their table, noticing the large beef pizza in the middle. Max inhaled, getting the scent of meat. He licked his lips, setting his cup down on the table.

"I paid, so dibs on the first slice," Max said, pulling a warm pizza slice from the round pizza.

The others dug in, grabbing slices. Max took a bite, savoring the seasoned juicy pizza. *Oh, man*, Max thought, closing his eyes. *Why don't I come here more often with Mom?*

He finished the slice in no more than ten bites and grabbed another one. He took a sip of the pineapple soda to wash the pizza down, taking another bite. Then out of the corner of his eye, Max saw a black figure standing outside. Finishing his pizza slice and wiping his hands on a napkin, Max walked out of Domino's.

Now outside, he sensed a presence somewhere behind him, so he took four steps forward and turned around. Strangely, he saw nothing. Max slowly turned back around, restless. A few moments passed, and his neck hairs stood on end. He felt a slight movement and turned around before summoning fire tendrils from the ground. A small scream issued from somewhere behind him.

Max saw a teenage girl in a typical emo attire tangled upside down in the tendrils. She had her hair dyed black and wore a black T-shirt and tight black jeans with a matching black cloak. Suddenly she wrapped herself in her cloak and reappeared behind him.

"Look, I don't want to fight you. Who are you?" Max asked.

The young woman kicked him in the stomach, and he doubled over in pain. Ashleigh and the others rushed out the door and spread around the teenager. She looked around and smirked, taking off her hood. "Four against one? I like my odds."

The girl spun around, and a pitch-black sword appeared in her hand. Just as the sword was about to hit Jessica, Damian jumped, creating a shield in midair. The impact shattered the ice and pushed the teen backward a bit. *Hmm*, she mused. *Master said you're hatchlings. You seem better than I bargained for.* She swung her sword at Max, and he barely rolled away.

Ashleigh called down lightning, aiming at the girl. Faster than the lightning itself, the teen raised the flat side of her sword and blocked it. A dark blast from the sword knocked Ashleigh off her feet. Damian fashioned a sword and shield of his own and ran at the teen. Just before Damian hit, the girl's sword turned into a lance and blocked Damian's sword. She stabbed at Damian's chest, and he blocked it with his shield.

Dark energy enveloped the emo teen, and her black aura grew around her, turning into a thirty-foot-tall version of herself. She floated at the heart of the aura and looked like a speck compared to it. A giant aura dagger appeared in the aura giant's hand. She threw it savagely at the kids, and they rolled out of the way, barely in time. Ashleigh called down lightning on herself, and electricity arched and jumped around her.

Ashleigh dashed at her, zipping in between her legs at eight hundred miles an hour.

"Argh!" the giant emo teenage aura screamed in frustration. Ashleigh taunted her, sticking out her tongue and wiggling her fingers at her. The aura chased after her, cracking the ground wherever she stepped. The loud noises attracted a crowd of people who watched the scene intently, trying to figure out exactly what was going on.

"Damian, can you try the aura?" Max asked desperately. Damian nodded and sat cross-legged on the ground. Ice and snow floated around him, and Jessica and Max took a step back, cautious. The air chilled around Damian and a blue glowing energy pulsed through his body. A turquoise-blue aura surrounded him. He floated up as the aura grew—head, arms, chest, and legs forming. Damian floated to the nose part of the aura, looking like a blue dot compared to the approximately nine-meter-tall figure surrounding him. A giant blue cape billowed behind him. The aura hovered above the ground for a few seconds, scanning its surroundings.

Aura-Damian launched himself down the street, Jessica and Max in tow. The two quickly gave up after he rounded the corner.

"Are we gonna catch up to him?" Jessica asked.

"Nope."

Damian's eyes scanned the buildings for a sign of the giant black aura. Ashleigh really needed to get away; otherwise, she'd probably meet a very sticky end. But emo teen found Damian first. She slammed into him from behind, knocking him to the ground. He crushed several hover cars in the act of falling, their alarms blaring. Picking himself up, he fashioned an aura-filled throwing knife in his right hand and drew his hand back. He threw it with all the force in his giant aura's hand and stood still.

The emo's aura deflected it without a scratch and gave Damian an uppercut. Honestly, he pictured it going differently. He landed with a thud on the ground. The real him took no damage, but his aura cracked the ground with the force of the fall. As he tried to stand, someone made a surprise save. He felt something speed past his ear and looked up. Ashleigh had a giant yellow aura around her and had slammed into the teen at just a little more than Mach 1, the speed of sound. Many surrounding buildings were severely damaged from the sonic boom that occurred, and Damian himself was knocked down. *Such destructive power*, Damian thought.

As Damian tried once again to stand, he pictured Ashleigh's thoughts running along these lines: *Newsflash! Emo kid destroys half the city! Oh, I can't let that happen.*

Damian got up and surveyed his surroundings. From the looks of it, Ashleigh had slammed the teen into a building. Rubble and shattered glass were scattered all over the ground.

Ashleigh's aura blasted the teen with a large beam of electricity, and her black aura faded. Jessica and Max appeared next to Ashleigh and tied up the teen with ropes of their respective elements. Damian's aura disappeared, and he ran over to where everyone was. Ashleigh's aura disappeared, and she fell to her knees, exhausted.

Max helped her up, and they untied the teenage girl. "Fly back to your 'master' and tell him that he should try us again and see what we do."

The teenager nodded and covered herself in her cloak, uttering the words, "Until we meet again." She disappeared in a surge of dark energy.

"Guys, are you feeling the pattern here?" Damian asked.

"Yeah," Max replied, "I've been feeling it too. First a guy with the power to turn people into aliens—on a large scale too."

"Then a teenage girl with dark-energy abilities, and not only that, but she said she had a master somewhere," Damian continued.

"And don't forget the lights above us when we got our powers," Ashleigh and Jessica finished.

26

"Wait, you saw it too?" Max asked, bewildered.

They nodded.

"What does it mean, though?" Damian asked.

"It means that this was all someone's master plan," Max concluded, punching his fist into his open palm.

The tension in the air could have been cut with a knife. Max's terrifying words sank in. "So you're saying…," Ashleigh started.

"That someone's behind all this?" Jessica finished.

"Nice find, Sherlock," Damian said sarcastically. "Yes, someone's behind this."

"Luckily, he's right here for you to find," a voice said from behind them.

There was a sucking sound, and Damian found himself being dragged into an orange portal. The four friends grabbed one another's hands, and Max linked them together. He tried to fly away, but the vortex was stronger; he had only learned how to fly a few hours ago. Jessica created a water whip and flung it at a pole. It wrapped around it, giving her hope that they'd be able to escape. But the orange vortex sucked them in, along with the pole.

"Goodbye, world," Damian whispered as they were sucked into oblivion.

CHAPTER 4

Jessica Names a Serial Killer!

Never fall into fiery portals to oblivion. Jessica's body screamed in pain as she smashed boulder after boulder after boulder. She tried to slow her fall with water, but it kept evaporating. After fifteen seconds of excruciating pain, Jessica finally hit the ground, her fall stopped. Her back felt like it had broken into a quadrillion pieces, and she felt very dizzy. Her breathing was labored, but she managed to stand up. She looked around and felt something breathe on her neck. Jessica turned around, terrified. The moment she finished her motion, she was slammed with a clawed fist. She flew into a nearby boulder as the creature bounded after her.

Jessica jumped out of the way of the creature, hitting it in the head with her fist. Unfortunately, her fist didn't do a thing; it simply bounced off the creature's hide. The creature roared and ran at her, claws out. Instinctively, she ran full speed away from the creature, but it was fast. Jessica rounded a corner and hid behind a boulder. The creature ran away in search of her. *Phew*, she thought. *That was close.* But now she had to get to her friends. She jumped onto a boulder to look for them and found Damian straight across from her.

Jessica ran like a madman toward Damian and hid behind a boulder just for the sake of sneaking up on him. She got behind him and punched his shoulder lightly. He tensed and turned, only to find her behind him. He let out a deep breath and relaxed his fist, dropping the remnants of a rock. Jessica made a mental note not to get on Damian's bad side. They ran off to find the other two but were thwarted by a group of fiery monsters, a spiky creature, and some red jellyfish that were sparking red electricity.

Jessica guessed she shouldn't have been so surprised that the giant jellyfish attacked first. They wrapped her and Damian with their tentacles and shocked them. Jessica shot water. It evaporated, but it had the effect she wanted. The evaporated water made the air moist and short-circuited the jellyfish. The spiky creature ran at Damian and Jessica and tried to hit them, but they were quick. Damian came behind it, and Jessica distracted it in front. Damian found its underside and scratched it. The monster turned around and tried to bite him, only to have a fist break its jaw. Twelve more of the monsters came back and started biting and snapping at the pair.

Jessica shot water into the hot air, and it turned to mist. The air got foggy, and Damian used that chance to knock all of them out. When the mist cleared, all Jessica saw was spiky waste and rings of fire around and above them. But something was wrong: the fire rings were moving. Then she figured it out: they were the fire creatures. They charged, and Jessica spun around while shooting water. It turned into a mist vortex. She managed to put a water ball inside it to sustain it, and it shielded them from sight, but took most of her energy because she had already used up a lot of it.

Jessica dropped to the ground, panting, and Damian carried her away. The water ball exploded, and then the vortex exploded and dampened the creatures' fires. Damian hid her behind a boulder and created a flurry of snow and ice. The ice turned to water and cooled her down as she got up. She saw the fire creatures flying away and eased a bit. Damian and Jessica walked a bit more and got surrounded by blue gas. *Seriously, what does it take to not get attacked these days!* Jessica thought.

She took one breath of air and wished she hadn't. It smelled like chlorine mixed with rotten eggs. Damian collapsed, and Jessica shot water, which turned to mist, at the blue wall of gas. The mist went inside the gas, and it glowed. Jessica saw red eyes. For a second, she thought it was Max; but when the monster stepped out, she nearly passed out from fear.

The monster had black scales, four stingers, two red eyes, eight legs, a pair of wings, and razor-sharp claws. Jessica decided to call it the scorpion! No. The dragon! No…Ultrabeast! Yeah. It was the ultimate combination of scary beasts. The reeking gas went away, and the Ultrabeast stepped toward Jessica. When it got close enough, it growled in its throat and raised one of its stingers. Jessica didn't know how long those stingers were until she got close. Jessica, frozen in panic, didn't move as it picked her up with its tail and looked at her.

Jessica desperately thought about anything that would get her out of the clutches of the Ultrabeast. *How about your powers, dummy?* said something inside of her. *Right*, she thought. She shot water from her hands, the water turning to steam the moment it left her body. Her hands were steaming from her evaporated water, scaring the Ultrabeast. It looked down at Jessica's hands and dropped her. As soon as she hit the ground, it lashed out with its stinger. Jessica rolled away, picked Damian up, and ran for dear life. The Ultrabeast unfolded its black wings and flew after her, creating a powerful gust of wind as it lifted off the ground. It easily caught up with them and tripped Jessica with its tail. She rolled over, and Damian fell out of her arms and rolled to the ground.

The Ultrabeast saw him and opened its mouth, revealing five rows of twenty-four sharp teeth. It lunged at Damian, and he quickly woke up and jumped onto its head and hit it while it roared. Jessica guessed Max and Ashleigh heard the roar because a minute later, they were there. Ashleigh struck at its legs, and Max distracted it with fire juggling.

Max kept juggling and finally launched the fireballs at the Ultrabeast. The hit left it dazed and also left an opening for them to strike. Ashleigh threw a ball of electricity, and Max shot a fireball. Damian made an ice shield before they collided and blew up on the Ultrabeast, sending it into the ground. The kids let their guard down, thinking they'd won, but the creature stung Jessica's leg before it disappeared in the blue gas, growling.

Jessica, acting on an instinct she didn't know she had, used her water to clean the wound and take out the venom, but the wound was still visible. Well, at least she wasn't going to die from the venom.

"What was that thing!" screamed Ashleigh.

"That *thing* is the Ultrabeast," Jessica said.

"How do you know?" Ashleigh asked.

"I know because I named it," Jessica said proudly.

Ashleigh just rolled her eyes. The skin around Jessica's wound was already starting to scar, surprising everyone around her.

Wow, Max mused, *enhanced healing factor.*

"All right, maybe we should split up to view this area," Ashleigh suggested.

Max frowned, saying, "Shouldn't we stick together? It'd be easier to defend ourselves that way."

"Don't worry. We'll go in teams of two," Ashleigh said, convincing Max.

"All right. Who goes with who?" Max asked.

"How about me and Damian, and you and Ashleigh?" Jessica proposed.

"Sure. Let's go!" Max said, running in the left direction with Ashleigh in tow.

"Since they took left, we take right!" Jessica said, taking off to the right. Damian grinned, running after her.

After a few hot, sweaty minutes, Max and Ashleigh stopped running. Ashleigh dropped to her knees, panting. "Even with our enhanced recovery, running at that speed, at that long a distance, in this heat!"

Max turned around, wanting to survey the land behind them. But when he looked behind, he saw a black creature with wings, razor-sharp claws, two red eyes, and four stingers. "Ashleigh, turn around and look at this," he said.

Ashleigh turned around, trying to figure out what Max was talking about. When she spotted the Ultrabeast, she gasped. They looked closer and saw it fighting off twelve fiery creatures. They were named sun dragons for their fiery abilities. The sun dragons split up into two groups: ones that made a fire ring above the Ultrabeast and ones that circled it. The dragons breathed fire at one another, and when the fires came together, they made a smoke ring around the Ultrabeast.

The Ultrabeast opened its mouth and shot a green blast in a circle around it. The green beam missed the sun dragons, and they shot fire back at the Ultrabeast. The Ultrabeast opened its mouth, swallowed the fire, and shot the green stuff back at them. This time, the green beam collided with five of them and sent them flying through the air, into boulders, and off a cliff. The remaining seven scratched and bit at the Ultrabeast, but its scales protected it.

The Ultrabeast flew up with unnatural speed and stopped abruptly, which shook the dragons off the Ultrabeast and down to the hard ground. The dragons got up and flew toward the Ultrabeast, preparing to breathe fire. The Ultrabeast stopped and wrapped its tails around the dragons, shaking them around.

The dragons breathed fire frantically, making the Ultrabeast let go of them. The dragons screeched again, and five more dragons appeared, then ten, then twenty, then forty! Forty dragons circled the Ultrabeast, breathing fire nonstop. The Ultrabeast flew up toward the cliff without knowing the trap it was flying into. The sun dragons followed, chasing the Ultrabeast toward the cliff.

When the Ultrabeast got to the cliff, it waited for the sun dragons to come close. Once the dragons got close, it dove with speed, hoping to outfly them. But the dragons were faster and soon were at the Ultrabeast's tails. Then the Ultrabeast spread its wings, caught air, and soared up, leaving the sun dragons to plummet to their deaths.

That's when the trap sprang. A hundred more sun dragons came flying and breathing fire at the Ultrabeast. It was caught off guard and hit by multiple beams of fire. It recovered quickly and blasted its green beam in a circle. The blast hit fifty of them, and they fell down to the bottom of the cliff. The Ultrabeast opened its mouth and shot down the remaining ones.

There were only four dragons that escaped—too easy for the Ultrabeast. It taunted the sun dragons by wagging tails in their faces and making them come closer. Then as quick as lightning, the Ultrabeast struck all four of them in the wings with its stingers. They started to flap frantically, the venom already acting. That was when the Ultrabeast made its final move. It struck them in their heads and shook its stingers inside them to release all the venom. The sun dragons went limp and fell to the bottom of the cliff.

The Ultrabeast caught three of them in its tails and flew over the cliff, going into a hole with their bodies. Max gestured for Ashleigh to grab his hand, and he flew the two of them after the Ultrabeast. But first, thinking of how they were going to appeal to the Ultrabeast, Max flew them to the bottom of the cliff. They quickly picked up two more sun dragons and flew over the cliff into the hole that the Ultrabeast flew into. They heard the sickening crunch of bones being chewed and eaten and followed the sound into a chamber lit up with the light of fire.

In the middle of the fire sat the Ultrabeast, chewing on dragon bones. The Ultrabeast saw them, and they froze. It set down its bones that it was chewing on and stalked toward the two. It opened its mouth and lit it up with its green, glowing substance. They got a full view of its 120 teeth as it raised up one of the sun dragons.

The Ultrabeast opened its mouth and ate the sun dragon. Max gave it the second one, and it gobbled it up. It looked at them and made a gurgling sound. Then they heard a loud roar, and the Ultrabeast growled and roared back. Then they saw just what it was roaring at. From the lightly illuminated cave and the bright light shining from outside, they could make out the silhouette of a dragon. The dragon ran away but kept roaring at the Ultrabeast from wherever it was.

Meanwhile, Jessica and Damian stopped in their tracks, pausing to take a break. They'd walked in circles and encountered so many of these red snakelike creatures that happened to be able to spit venom. But now they were exhausted and sweating profusely.

"I never thought I'd say it, but I'm starting to hate the warmth," Damian said. "Sure, I like being warm, but this place is just a no-no!" he exclaimed.

Jessica nodded in agreement and didn't talk, wanting to save her energy. But then they heard a loud roar, and they froze. They turned to where the sound came from and got up, running toward it. They found a hole and jumped inside.

They found a chamber lit by green fire and littered with bones. They then saw the Ultrabeast, Ashleigh, and Max. The Ultrabeast was roaring and growling ferociously. Then it flew out of the hole and into the open sky. There was no way Jessica and Damian weren't going to follow it, so they climbed back up the hole and found the Ultrabeast facing off against the largest sun dragon they'd ever seen. It was as long as three regular sun dragons, and its wings were as long as three wings on each side.

Damian could only hope that he was wrong when he said it was the queen sun dragon. The Ultrabeast roared and tried to scratch the Queen. She moved out of the way and shot red, white, and blue fire at the Ultrabeast. Dodging it, the Ultrabeast blasted the Queen with its green fire. The Queen got hit but stayed standing. The Queen made a hissing sound and spat a blue liquid onto the ground. The liquid grew into a blue version of the Ultrabeast, except it had green eyes and a red fire blast.

The two Ultrabeasts faced off against each other with green and red fire. The Queen jumped on the original Ultrabeast and breathed fire in its face, hoping to burn some scales. She bit the Ultrabeast on the neck and broke through its scales, injuring it minorly. The Ultrabeast opened its mouth and shot a dark-green combination of fire and acid at the Queen's wing. The combo burned a hole through the right wing of the Queen, rendering her unable to fly. She scurried around on the ground, shooting fireballs wherever she wanted; but when the Ultrabeast found the kids behind it, they decided it was time to leave.

Jessica and Damian crawled back to the hole, calling Ashleigh and Max out.

"Let's go," Jessica said.

"But how are we going to get out of here?" Max asked. "We don't have the power to travel through dimensions."

"Like this!" called a voice. A blue portal appeared near the four kids, and they were sucked in again.

"Dang it!" Ashleigh shouted angrily, cursing her inability to create dimensional portals. They at least hoped the portal would take them back to Earth, but their luck wasn't very good at this point.

When the kids finally were dumped out of the portal, they nearly wet their pants from the sight they saw.

CHAPTER 5

We Saved a Totally Human Alien! Yay!

Giant monster?

Expectation: Max can take care of it!

Reality: Max is peeing his pants right now!

The monster had a snake body with horns and had a tail, but four wings were sticking out from its sides, and it had four clawed legs. It turned its head toward the kids and roared. It then flew over to a glacier and hissed. The kids noticed that, one, their environment was freezing. Both literally and metaphorically. Two, they were surrounded by blue snakes and white spiders that were just going around doing their business. And three, the place looked like Antarctica.

The moment the monster roared, the animals stopped what they were doing and shook from side to side. *That's weird*, thought Ashleigh. Max looked at Damian, Jessica, and Ashleigh, and they all started to back away. The beast looked at them and hissed, causing the animals to stalk toward them. Max made fireballs and juggled them. The animals stared at the light of the fire and then resumed progressing. The blue snakes revealed wings and took off toward them. Max threw a fireball at one, and it turned to steam.

The rest of the creatures charged the kids, and Damian wasted no time. He forged an ice sword and threw it horizontally. The sword hit five of the snakes, and they turned to snow. Ashleigh had a bit of trouble summoning lightning. The air was so cold that she couldn't create enough heat friction to call down her lightning. Max had to shoot fire into the air to create heat for her. She finally made a ball of electricity and threw it at the monster dad.

The lightning ball hit it in the chest and sent it sprawling on the ground. It hissed, and the spiders bit and spit venom at them in retribution. They made balls of webbing and chucked them. As much as Max hated to admit it, Damian was the most powerful one here. He had ice powers, and this place was full of ice. Damian threw a torrent of daggers, and when that didn't work, he slammed his fists on the ice and created a hole where the spiders were. The spiders fell into the hole, and Damian closed it. He surrounded himself with ice and rose up. He started flying toward the giant monster at impressively high speeds. *When did he learn to fly!* the others thought.

The water surrounding the glacier was turned to ice because of Damian's flying. He flew straight into the giant monster king and pushed him off the glacier, destroying said glacier with the force of the hit. He curved in the air and shot back down at the monster king only to meet a tail whip. The tail threw Damian into the water under the ice of the ocean, and the king roared.

Max thought Damian wouldn't come out of the water, but it turned sky blue and froze. Then they saw him come out. He was glowing sky blue and was angry—really angry. Think of a polar bear that lost her cubs. Now multiply that by five, and you got Damian. He slammed his fists into the king and threw it into the water. Damian flew into the water and pushed the monster king as far as he could go into the ocean, sealing him with ice.

He came back up and froze the water so the beast couldn't get out. He flew back to the kids and landed, glowing brighter than a floodlight in the dark. Max had to cover his eyes to protect them from the brightness of his glowing, lest he went blind. Damian stopped shining after a couple seconds and promptly fainted. Jessica caught him and set him down to have a look at him. Then something on a faraway glacier caught Max's eye—a green ice block. Ashleigh noticed it too, looking at Max.

Max lifted Ashleigh into the air and smoothly flew to the glacier. They dropped to the ground and walked over to the ice. It glowed green and cracked a bit. Ashleigh noticed that there were several other cracks in it. But she thought about it harder and realized something. "Max," she whispered, "I think something's in there."

Max nodded and took two steps back. A fireball grew in his hands, and he unleashed it on the ice. Normally, the ice would have melted, but it was supercold there. Max kept at it, making sure the melting water didn't refreeze. Finally, it all melted and revealed a boy just an inch taller than Max. His hair and hands were glowing green. He fell facedown on the ground, and Max tried to feel his pulse as he stopped glowing. He could feel it steadily beating, and he was breathing as well.

Max picked him and Ashleigh up and flew back to Damian and Jessica. Max set the boy down on the ice, and Damian stirred. Ignoring Damian, Jessica felt the boy's forehead and looked up, deciding what to do next. She drew a small amount of cold water from the ocean, and Max heated it up. She spread the now warm water on the boy's head, and his eyes flickered open.

The kid got up, stared at the four, and glowed green. Max looked at himself and noticed that he was glowing orange. Jessica was glowing royal blue, Damian was glowing sky blue, and Ashleigh was glowing bright yellow. Max made a fireball and rose into the air, preparing to defend himself, but the kid knocked him out of the sky with a single green blast.

Max did a backflip in the air and flew at the kid. He shot another beam, and Max deflected it with a blast of fire. Max picked him up and threw him into the sky, preparing a fireball. The kid created a surfboard out of plants to fly and shot energy blasts at Max. Ashleigh made a ball of electricity and shot it at the boy, wanting to protect her teammate. He dodged and sent a powerful blast of energy at her, knocking her into the ocean. Max jumped after her and brought her out, hovering just above the water.

Ashleigh pushed Max off and flew up above the boy, threw him into the ocean with her fist, and shot a continuous beam of electricity at the water. She turned her back on him, letting her guard down, and he rose out of the ocean and slammed into her. She fell out of the sky, and Max caught her just before she hit the surface of the ocean. Max flew her to Jessica and Damian and stormed back out.

Max flew over the ocean and scanned for the boy, who was flying on his surfboard straight toward him. Max shot fire at him, and it hit the boy, sending him flying into a glacier. He flew out and brought rocks with him. He threw a boulder at Max, who punched it back. The punch left a glowing red mark that blew up in the boy's face as the rock flew back to him. Unfazed, the boy threw the remaining rocks at Max, and he was nearly pummeled to death, but an ice shield saved him. Max flew back to the ice where Jessica and Ashleigh were, and Damian met him there. The boy brought hundreds of stones with him, and Damian made a protective ice dome. Then the boy made a giant fist out of all the stones and started to smash the shield.

The ice started cracking, and Jessica finished healing Ashleigh. Ashleigh got up and touched the shield, electrifying it. Damian took all the ice, forming a sphere, and blasted the boy with it. He dodged it and landed on the ice. He then started to walk over to the group.

"Sorry about that," the boy said. "I didn't mean any harm. I just feared for my life, that's all. By the way, my name's Connor."

He asked them for their names, and they told him.

"Max," Max said.

"Damian," Damian said.

"Jessica," Jessica replied.

"And last, but definitely not least, Ashleigh," Ashleigh said, smirking at her own antics.

Connor nodded. "I suggest we get out of here, though. It can get colder than this, ya know." They all agreed and tried to find a portal.

"Yeah, we need a portal to Earth," Max said sheepishly, rubbing his head. Connor grinned and shot a blast of dark-green energy at the ground, which turned into a portal.

They all jumped through the portal and found themselves in outer space with no space gear. They started to clutch their necks, thinking they'd suffocate, and flew to Earth at hypersonic speed. Ignoring the bright stars moving past them in the distance, they broke the sound barrier and soon broke through Earth's atmosphere. They started to choke, but this motivated them to move faster.

Max specifically was flying so fast that onlookers only saw a dot of red and a trail of smoke when he flew past them. They followed the smoke trail, and he hit the ground.

Max tried to stop flying, but that was kind of hard considering that he was flying ten times faster than the speed of sound. People flocked to the crater that he made when he hit the ground, and they picked him up. Ashleigh saw them take him, and she called the others. They flew after him, and she grabbed him away. She set Max down, and he got up, looking around for any store where he could buy a drink.

But they had no time for rest as Max heard an explosion and looked up into the sky. He saw Universal Labs jets in the sky flying toward them. He flew up and blasted one of the jets with fire, remembering his horrible experience with Universal Labs. It blew up, and twelve people parachuted to the ground. They had special gear made to withstand the kids' powers, and they had laser guns—cool but not cool at the same time.

Max led them to Damian and the rest, whistling to get his friends to help. Connor and Damian created a barrier by combining the elements of earth and ice. The barrier blocked the laser beams and gave Ashleigh and Jessica time to plan their attack. The girls told the boys to get out of the way, and they got out. Jessica drew water from the Atlantic Ocean twenty meters away, and Ashleigh sparked the water. The electricity flowed through the water and shocked the people with the lasers.

Meanwhile, Max flew around the jets in the air while shooting fire at the same time, and he made a fire tornado. The jets were pulled by the tornado, and Max prepared to destroy them. He pulled all the fire into a giant fireball and held it there before throwing it at the jets and blowing them up.

Max flew down to help Connor and Damian and added fire to the elemental wall. Ashleigh and Jessica soon added lightning and water to the wall. They pushed the wall toward the dozens of people with laser guns who were attacking and threw them into the ocean because that's what civil people do. Ashleigh jumped into the water, zapped the whole thing, and flew right back out like nothing ever happened.

The people struggled to get up and out of the ocean, for electrocution was *not* a helpful thing. Jessica made the waves grow more powerful, drowning the evil Universal Labs members. But oh well—they were evil. Jessica raised her hands, and the ocean rose up. She let her hands fall to her sides, and the ocean backed down.

"I think we deserve a break," Max said cheerfully. "Let's get some ice cream."

The others shrugged, and they all flew away to Dairy Queen for a snack.

But when they got there, Dairy Queen was empty. There were no managers, no customers, and no employees—the place was just deserted. The group walked farther inside, but there were no people, just overturned tables and cracked trays. Wait, cracked trays? That wasn't right. There were supposed to be neat tables and intact trays, not a destroyed, ghosted building.

They walked into the kitchen and saw a horrifying ice beast. It was twelve feet long with icy claws and four jaws. It had pincers on its head and eight legs. Max looked at its tail and saw spikes sticking out, ready to be released. "What the heck is *that*!" Ashleigh yelled, hands sparking.

The beast turned its head toward the kids and curled its tail. It released its spikes almost faster than the kids could react, but Damian was quicker. He made a shield and blocked the spikes. The monster roared and sent sound waves everywhere. The piercing waves made Damian drop the shield, and it clattered to the ground, shattering. The monster lashed out with its claws, but Max met its icy claws with his fiery fist.

The entire building shook with the force of the hit. The beast released more spines, but Max blasted it with fire. Jessica made a water whip, and Ashleigh used electricity to make it spark. Jessica whipped the beast and wrapped the whip around it soon after. The electricity inside the whip shocked the beast and made it dig its legs into the floor.

"Sit, beast, sit!" Jessica ordered.

Max drew a fiery *M* in the air and threw it at the beast. The fire came in contact with its hide, and it started steaming. The creature released spines at Max, and he dodged all but one. The spine hit him in the leg and sent him sprawling on the ground. He pulled it out and groaned in pain.

Damian made a spear out of ice and threw it at the monster. It rolled out of the way of the spear and roared again. Max threw a weak fireball, and the beast deflected it with its tough hide. Then it charged the group with its pincers. It ran at them, still roaring, and nearly maimed Max, but he dodged just in time.

It stopped roaring and shot its spines at Max. Max dodged them, but his leg was bothering him. He did a backflip over the beast and onto its head and formed a fiery rope. He tied the rope around the beast's snout, and the rope started to burn it. It roared and shook its head, trying to throw him off.

Connor and Damian were trying to get a clear shot at the beast, but it was moving too fast for them to hit it without hitting Max. Max jumped up into the air and then slammed into the creature with all his might. He pushed it deeper and deeper into the earth.

As Max went farther down, he felt himself getting stronger. That was probably because he was getting close to magma. He used one last push and sent it deep down into the earth, farther than anyone had ever been before and farther than anyone would ever be. Max flew back up and closed the hole with Connor's help.

"That was harder than it should have been," Ashleigh said, breathing hard.

Max nodded. "You're right. We need to practice. I know just the place."

CHAPTER 6

Noran? What Kind of Name Is Noran?

You'd think that heroes of this caliber would need a professional training room, right? But nope—an abandoned shed would do just fine. When they landed, walking inside, Connor put up rock walls around the shed to prevent it from collapsing. It was *seriously old*. None of them wanted to have a shed collapsing on their heads, that was for sure. Anyway, Connor volunteered to be the "coach" and watch the match. He separated the room into four sides with walls and said that the walls would come down when the battle was about to begin. Max couldn't see what Jessica and Damian were doing, but he saw Ashleigh charge up with lightning from a starting storm outside.

Letting the walls down, Connor announced that the last two people standing would fight against each other, and then the winner would go against him.

"Are you now ready?" he asked.

Everyone nodded.

"All right. Begin!" He shouted for the match to start, and Max did a perfect 360-degree spin while shooting fireballs. Damian raised an ice shield and blocked some of them while Jessica got away from them by making a pool of water under her feet and disappearing inside it.

Jessica reappeared right next to Max and shot water in his face. Though the water blurred his vision, Max retaliated by making the pool of water under Jessica evaporate. He blasted her into the wall and turned around to face Damian. Max threw a blue fireball at him, and Damian put up his shield, but the fireball melted it and slammed into him. Damian threw a huge ball of snow and ice into the air and let it explode. Hail and snow started falling everywhere, making it hard to see with the thick white cover.

Damian played Max's blindness to his advantage, landing blows as Max struggled to spot him. Max blocked a hit and jumped back, making a fire sword, while Damian fashioned his own out of ice. The snow cover cleared, allowing them both to see better. Damian lunged for Max, who rolled under his feet, knocking him down. Now on the ground, Damian threw ice bombs, and they detonated in front of Max, clouding his field of vision once more. At this time in the battle, Max had forgotten that Ashleigh was still there, waiting for a moment to strike; and when he couldn't see, that's when she struck him with lightning. Max shriveled into the ground, defeated.

Now Ashleigh and Damian were the remaining two, the victors of this battle. Connor called for a break, and Jessica supplied Damian with water while Ashleigh called down more lightning from the storm and boosted her energy. Connor called them back after they were done resting and resumed the match. Damian attacked first with a spear, aiming straight at Ashleigh. She simply blocked it with a plasma shield, a plan formulating in her head. She threw the shield at Damian and then ignited it with lightning. Damian ducked under it, and Ashleigh outstretched her hand. It came back like a boomerang and slammed into his back while flying into Ashleigh's hand. Damian fell hard onto the floor just as she charged an electric beam, but he rolled out of the way just in time.

Damian rolled to his feet and created an ice spear before running at Ashleigh. She dodged it when he threw it and started to fly around him. Ashleigh blasted him with fast beams of electricity, giving him no time to react. Damian formed a shield and tried to block them, but he wasn't focused enough, and the shield broke, sending him flying backward.

Ashleigh smirked and dropped to the ground, sprinting toward Damian. She formed a small blade out of electricity and moved behind Damian, keeping the weapon just above his head. "I win," Ashleigh said quietly.

Damian raised his hands in surrender, and Ashleigh moved the blade away from him, letting its energy dissipate.

"Get ready," Connor called to Ashleigh.

She nodded and channeled lightning from the storm again, charging herself like a battery.

Damian stood up, panting. Walking to Max, he gasped. "Dude, your girlfriend is—"

Max gave him a sharp kick to his left leg, rendering him unable to walk. "Never mind. But she's good. Coming from me, that's a major compliment."

"Shut up and watch the game," Max said, but Damian could see a tiny smile dancing on his lips.

Connor and Ashleigh walked across from each other, preparing to begin. "Let's go!" Jessica called, and the two began.

Connor made tiny rocks in the shape of bullets and fired them straight at Ashleigh. Her plasma shield appeared in her hand, and she blocked the rocks. Then she threw the shield at Connor, and he ducked under it. It boomeranged back at Connor, but he grabbed it while it was in midair without even glancing at it. Ashleigh, not wanting Connor to use her shield against her, separated the molecules and atoms in the shield, and it disappeared. With a flick of his hand, Connor made vines grow around Ashleigh, and they entangled her, rendering her immobile.

"You're stuck in my web now," Connor remarked.

Realizing she was trapped, Ashleigh closed her eyes and imagined her element, lightning, surrounding her and breaking her free of her restraints. A spark flickered beside her. Then another, and another, and another! In only a few seconds, electricity surrounded Ashleigh and obliterated the vines. Now free, she slammed her fists together, and an electric shock wave knocked Connor off his feet. Connor, landing on his feet, raised boulders and threw them at Ashleigh, but she sliced them in half every single time.

All right, Connor thought, *this might not be as easy as I previously assumed.*

Ashleigh rushed at Connor, creating two long swords in her hands. Connor shifted his footing and pressed his palms on the ground, expression serious. Earthen spikes erupted out of the ground, snaking toward Ashleigh. *Too easy*, she thought.

Ashleigh flew into the air above the spikes, grinning to herself. But Connor already had a plan. The spikes raised themselves higher, getting scarily close to Ashleigh. *What?* Ashleigh thought. She charged a beam of electricity and fired it at the closest spike to her. The spike was destroyed, but Ashleigh had only just begun to deal with them. *I'll have to get to the ground*, she thought. *If I stay up here, I'll have a better chance of getting impaled. But if I'm on the ground, I have better maneuverability.* Ashleigh abruptly stopped flying, dropping to the ground.

Ashleigh dashed toward Connor, weaving around spikes sticking out of the ground. Connor ran at her, forming a shield out of the ground around him. Ashleigh formed a sword out of electricity and prepared to attack. The two met each other in the middle of the field, weapons clashing. Ashleigh made a quick slash at Connor with her sword, but he blocked it with his shield, shoving her backward. Connor quickly placed his hands on the ground, and restraints made of rocks and vines pinned her down. *Darn*, Ashleigh thought.

Ashleigh struggled and struggled but knew that she couldn't escape the hard vines that entangled her. She huffed, stopping her movements.

"Looks like I win," Connor said, releasing Ashleigh's restraints.

Ashleigh quietly stood up, rubbing her wrists and ankles. "I want to be that good," she muttered to herself. But then the building shook, and lightning flashed.

"What the—"

Max was cut off by loud, rumbling thunder. "We should probably check that out."

The others nodded in agreement, following Max as he ran out into the open.

The storm, which had started out as a regular rain and a bit of wind with a few flashes of lightning, had increased to tornadoes, floods, and lightning everywhere. Connor placed his hands on the ground, and earthen harnesses held all the kids down. The raging winds and floods would have washed them away had he not.

Suddenly a gray figure shot past the five. Connor noticed the figure first, releasing his restraints and flying after it. The others broke out of theirs, following Connor. Damian, thinking on his feet, made a wall of ice in front of the figure, and it slammed into the ice. Prepared to defend themselves, the group landed in front of the gray figure and discovered that it was not at all a "thing"—it was a boy. He had jet-black hair and a gray outfit that matched the color of his eyes.

He got up and ran quickly around the kids in circles, so fast that they couldn't keep up with him. Ashleigh, black hair flying in the wind, threw a ball of lightning at the boy, and he fell to the ground. "What's your name?" she asked him, hands sparking.

"My name is… ah… Noran," he said, eyes darting around to look for an escape route.

"Noran?" Damian chuckled. "What kind of name is Noran?"

Then Noran's leg twitched; Damian noticed it. Right before Noran could dash away, four ice walls appeared around him, closing all exits. "Nice try," Damian said, crossing his arms.

Noran huffed from inside his icy containment. "All right, I'm going out on a limb, but I'm going to assume you guys aren't evil."

Max frowned. "Why would you think we are evil?"

Noran quickly thought of an experience he'd had a few days before. "Let's just say I've had some bad experiences."

Damian, convinced, lowered the walls around Noran and helped him up. "Follow me," he said.

Ashleigh and Damian shrugged, preparing to follow. Max frowned. "Isn't that a bad idea?"

"At least he isn't trying to kill us," Jessica reasoned. Max nodded in agreement, turning to face Noran. He zoomed off, and the kids flew behind him.

He stopped at the Empire State Building and gestured for them to follow him up. He ran up the building while they flew up to the top, rain pouring on them. By the time they got to the top of the building, they were soaking wet. But when they saw some masked man creating giant thunderclouds, they had to use all the self-control they could muster to keep themselves from laughing. It was just ridiculous. He didn't even look like a decent villain.

He released the thunderclouds and turned to look at the group. He was nearly six feet tall and wore an antique black leather fencing jacket with a golden cloud necklace. He saw Noran and huffed in frustration. "What does it take for a villain to do things in peace?" he complained.

"Villain?" Noran snorted. "If you're going to be a villain, at least *look* the part!"

"Our friend here has a point," Connor added, getting nods from the others.

The man narrowed his eyes, and clouds flew right above the others' heads. Noran waved his hands at the clouds, and they were obliterated by a powerful gust of wind.

Noran drew more wind from the storm and aimed it at the man, trying to push him back, but he phased right through it. Connor raised the ground below his feet, but he turned intangible a second time and walked right through it. He turned tangible again and moved his arm in a sweeping motion. A violent gust of wind shoved the group off the building. Two vines shot out of Connor's hands. One vine grappled the ledge of the Empire State Building, and the other wrapped itself around the rest of them. Slightly straining his muscles, he swung them back onto the building.

Using only thought, Ashleigh called down lightning. At first, they just heard thunder (which actually came from a completely unrelated burst of lightning), but then an arc of lightning flashed down from the sky and crashed right on top of the villain. When the lightning fizzled away, the only thing that remained was a golden cloud necklace. The air smelled like barbecue. But at least the villain was gone, so the storms had stopped.

It was only now that Ashleigh took a moment to look at the destruction. The damage in New York was devastating. There were destroyed cars and buildings scattered on the ground, and people and police were panicking. "I'll need some molten sand," Noran said.

Connor created a huge earthen bucket, filling it with sand. Max grinned, keeping a steady blue flame on it. The sand melted, the heat creating molten sand. Connor created another bucket full of sand, and Max melted it. Soon enough, the two finished.

"Done," Max said, handing the buckets to Noran.

Noran zoomed down the building and ran around the city, fixing the damage he could fix as he ran. He came back to Connor and Max several more times for more molten sand. By the time he was done (which was seven minutes later), the city was, for the most part, repaired. The glass was (mostly) new and sparkly, the flooded ground had been stripped of its overflowing water, etc. But the cars…Noran couldn't do anything about that. Noran ran back up the Empire State Building, meeting the group again. They stared at him in amazement, and he grinned.

"I did say I was quick." Then he paused, frowning. "Wait, did I?" Ashleigh giggled.

The group led Noran down the building. They flew down to their training shack and showed Noran their weapons. "These things are sharp and pack quite a punch," Ashleigh explained, standing up.

Noran picked up Damian's sword and muttered, "It's weighted pretty well and *would* really pack a punch." He threw the sword directly at Ashleigh.

Unfazed, Ashleigh flicked her hand into the air, and a sudden blast of electric energy pushed the sword away. Noran stared at her, scrutinizing. He ran around her in quick circles, but she was prepared for this and sent multiple beams of electricity flying at the blur called Noran. They knocked him down, but he got right back up and grabbed the ice sword. He ran toward Ashleigh, and she put up a plasma shield. He ran into the shield, and she pushed him back. He stood back up and zoomed underneath the shield, rolling under her legs and knocking her down.

Ashleigh put up an electric dome around herself and focused. Every electron in the shed and every tiny particle orbited her. The electric dome around her dissolved into tiny electrons and joined the ones already orbiting her. Her eyes turned neon yellow, and she grinned. Ashleigh stepped out of her spot, and Noran threw the sword at her. A beam of electricity knocked it away, and she took another step toward him.

A lance appeared in Ashleigh's right hand. It glowed yellow with electricity, sparks shooting off it. Noran grabbed the ice sword off the ground and charged her. She stopped walking and waited for him to get close. Once he did, she spun the lance and disarmed him, pointing the tip at him.

"Looks like I win," Ashleigh stated.

"No, you don't," Noran said. He disappeared into thin air. Playing on Ashleigh's confusion, he reappeared in front of her and kicked her straight into the wall. While she was down, he slashed the air, and a tornado formed in front of him. He stepped inside the tornado and closed his eyes. The tornado latched onto his back and then disappeared in his body.

Spikes formed on Noran's arms and legs, and his eyes turned gray. On his back was a pair of wings, and the wind around him was so powerful it nearly knocked Ashleigh off her feet. He ran toward her, and she flew into the air. He jumped up and tackled her in mid-air. He pushed her onto the ground, but she kicked him off, sending him into the wall.

Ashleigh threw a bolt of lightning at Noran, but the wind orbiting him pushed it away. Then he made a sword out of air and threw it at her chest. The air went right through her left lung and out through the other side, and it didn't do anything to her for the first few seconds. But after about three seconds, all the air in her lungs was sucked out, and she couldn't breathe. Ashleigh felt like she was suffocating.

Ashleigh clutched at her throat, trying to breathe, but she just couldn't. Whatever had happened was definitely powerful. After ten terrifying seconds, the effects wore off, and Ashleigh could breathe again. Max, Damian, Connor, and Jessica watched her from the wall. Noran walked up to Ashleigh and fist-bumped her. She smiled back and blinked. He was gone before she even opened her eyes. Damian stifled a laugh as she turned back toward him. She frowned and raised her eyebrows at him, and he just laughed at her.

"What's so funny?" Ashleigh asked.

Damian smiled. "You barely landed a hit on Noran, who looks like he's about our age. He threw you around like a rag doll, and even though you tried, you didn't stand a chance."

Ashleigh's face turned red, and Damian shrugged. Ashleigh pulled her arm back, preparing to throw her lance. Damian put up an ice wall, blocking the lance. He quickly flew above it, moving toward the middle of the space. Ashleigh followed him, charging her electric energy. She slammed the ground with her hands and created a shock wave, which Damian jumped over.

He put up an ice dome around himself, and Ashleigh hit it with her fist. She made a small crack in the middle but otherwise didn't leave a mark. Ashleigh then jumped backward, shooting a powerful beam of electricity at the spot. The beam made a hole in the dome, and she flew up into the air. She dropped down toward it and threw her fist at it, hitting Damian in the process. He fell backward but quickly got to his feet as Ashleigh wasn't relenting.

He flew dozens of meters back and placed his palms on the ground. A layer of ice spread from that spot on the ground, extending everywhere. Ashleigh, not expecting this, slipped on the ice, falling onto her back. She quickly created two daggers in her hands, sticking them into the ground. She used them to prop her up, and she did a backflip, sliding backward, but sticking the landing otherwise. She outstretched her arms, and the blades flew into them. "I guess playtime's over," she commented.

Damian grinned, and snow swirled around him. "You know it."

Ashleigh crossed her daggers to make an *X* shape, and electricity pulsed around her. Ashleigh's eyes glowed yellow, and the corner of her mouth went up as she crouched down. *Let's get this party started*, she thought.

Damian, on the other side of the space, prepared himself as well. His eyes glowed sky blue, and two swords made of ice appeared in his hands. He narrowed his eyes.

Ashleigh dashed toward Damian, the heat from the electricity around her melting the ice as she ran. Damian dropped his swords, forming a large shield in front of him. Ashleigh threw both daggers at the shield, and they made two small holes. Ashleigh then threw her fists at the spot, shattering it. Damian grabbed his swords out of the air as Ashleigh pulled her daggers out from a shard of ice. Damian launched himself at Ashleigh, slashing at her with one of his swords. Ashleigh blocked it with her daggers, jumping backward as he overpowered her.

Damian's pretty good, Ashleigh thought. *But what can he do against two of me?* Ashleigh charged her electric energy and closed her eyes, imagining a double of herself right in front of her. Electric energy flew around the space in front of her, constructing a figure. When Ashleigh opened her eyes, she saw herself. Without turning around, her clone said, "We're battling Damian, right?"

"Yep," Ashleigh replied. The clone nodded, zipping toward Damian. Ashleigh followed, running right beside her. "Take the left, and I'll take right," Ashleigh said.

The two split up, and Damian carefully watched them through the corners of his eyes. As they approached either side of him, he shifted his footing, slamming his swords into the ground. Wherever Ashleigh or her clone would step, an ice spike would shoot out of the ground. The two girls were caught off guard at first but quickly adapted to it.

"I have a plan," Ashleigh's clone said. "But it's going to require two more clones. And we need to put some space between us and Damian."

Ashleigh nodded, creating two more of herself. *I don't think I can make any more clones at this point, what with the amount of energy I'm expending,* she thought. Ashleigh's first clone began explaining her idea as they moved backward. When the clone was done, they all nodded and spread out. Ashleigh threw several balls of electricity at Damian, trying to get his attention off the ice mine. The strategy worked as Damian pulled his swords out of the ground and blocked the attack, deactivating the ice mine.

"Let's go," Ashleigh whispered, and they all glanced at one another, grinning. All of them wielded daggers as they ran forward.

They spread out around Damian, and the first clone said, "Now."

All the Ashleighs threw volleys of daggers at Damian. Damian used his swords to block them while the Ashleighs moved forward in a square formation. One clone kicked Damian into the air while another one jumped into the air and kicked him down. As he fell, the third clone threw a ball of electricity at him, and it collided, exploding. All three of the clones flew below him and kicked him up while the real Ashleigh was already on the ground below Damian, preparing a giant ball of electricity. *This is probably going to be my last attack before I need to either recharge or take a break*, she thought.

Damian, having just been assaulted from more or less all sides, couldn't dodge this attack. Ashleigh jumped up above him and twisted around, slamming the giant glowing ball into him. The force of it threw Damian to the ground, and Ashleigh followed him. The ball of electricity exploded on Damian, a huge cloud of dust and smoke erupting from the spot. Max and the rest rushed to the area, running through the dust cloud.

When the cloud cleared, they saw both Damian and Ashleigh collapsed on the ground. The two were at the center of a huge crater, both breathing slowly. "That was exhausting," Ashleigh said.

"Aye," Damian agreed. "And before you tell me to get up, you'd need to give me a couple minutes to recharge."

But before anyone could say or do anything, an earsplitting bang shook the building. "Seriously!" Damian and Ashleigh chorused. "Give us a break!"

The two slowly and shakily got to their feet, the others supporting them. "C'mon," Max said, leading the group out through the doors of the shed. Another deafening crash sounded, and the kids all looked up.

There was a whole fleet of giant aircrafts in the air, their colors ranging from dark brown to black, and military fighter jets were rushing toward them.

"Guys, let's go! We got a city to save!" Max said, flying toward the fleet.

"I swear, having superpowers is a curse," Ashleigh muttered, flying up into the air with Damian. At this point, despite her tiredness, she lifted herself up, running on adrenaline. Unbeknownst to her, her energy levels were already rising.

CHAPTER 7

....

Beware Aliens Bearing Gifts!

Jessica was lost in thought. It was as if she was practicing a speech intended for a doubting audience. *Now, before you say, "These guys are just kids! They can't possibly deal with an entire fleet of invading space-ships," let me tell you that with little control of our powers, we stopped a postapocalyptic alien invasion, beat a girl with complete control of her dark-energy powers, defeated multiple giant monsters in a day, and beat a guy with weather powers (and intangibility, though he was just a wannabe). Plus, we survived in those other weird dimensions. Kids can do anything. If that's not enough proof for you—*

"The alien ships look like they can carry lots of aliens," Connor belted out, jolting Jessica back to reality.

"Nice job, Sherlock," Jessica muttered.

"Who's Sherlock?" Connor asked.

"Never mind."

"We've reached the drones," Jessica noted.

Connor nodded.

"And how do you even know that they're alien ships?" Jessica added, arching her eyebrows.

Connor never got a chance to answer because they were suddenly pulled off course by a strong force in front of them. In desperation, Jessica threw a water chain at Connor. He grabbed it and fastened it to his waist as she did the same. But then Connor noticed

53

two purple swirling masses behind the fleet. *Portals?* he thought. *They've already advanced that much?*

Connor quickly analyzed the situation. *A portal is an energy-based creation,* he thought. *So disrupting the energy flow just enough should close it.* Connor outstretched both of his arms, and green, glowing balls of energy swirled in his hands. They slowly grew in size, soon becoming the size of giant beach balls. Connor launched them at the two portals, watching as the pull of the masses directed them in. The two energy balls disappeared inside the portals, and they started swirling rapidly, closing in on themselves. "Jessica!" Connor called to his teammate, creating a giant rock wall to shield them from the inevitable energy outpour of the closing.

Jessica got behind the shield right as both portals shut. A second passed, and all was calm. Then there was a loud roar sounding like the scream of wind in a tornado, and energy pulsed in all directions. A bad feeling settled in Connor's stomach, telling him that they wouldn't be completely safe behind the rocks. Then he heard something coming straight for them. "Duck!" he yelled, and the two lowered their heads.

A purple wave of energy sliced through the rock wall in the exact spot where their heads would have been. *I could have just died!* Jessica thought in fear.

Connor took down the rock wall, creating another big ball of energy in between his hand. "You might want to take a step back," he said.

"You don't know who you're talking to," Jessica stated.

Connor shrugged, rushing forward. He slammed the energy ball into the smallest spacecraft he could see. The green ball of energy obliterated the wing of the ship, sending it and the passengers spiraling down into the ocean. A trail of smoke was left in its wake. Connor repeated the process, destroying several more airships.

Jessica smiled to herself and raised both hands. The ocean rolled and tossed, and waves sank the debris of the fallen spacecrafts. She flew toward an airship and grinned. She drew water from the ocean below her and covered herself with it. She then flew straight through the aircraft, destroying the engine, controls, and all whatnot.

Meanwhile, Damian circled around an alien jet and bombarded it with beams of ice. Parts of it froze as he flew, and it spiraled down into the ocean. Max flew over one of the spaceships, trying to get to the biggest of them all. *If I take out the lead, the other ones will just be fodder*, he thought. But then several smaller aircrafts flew in around it, cutting Max off. They began firing what looked like beams of light at them, which Ashleigh and Max easily dodged. But Damian wasn't as lucky.

"Beware aliens bearing gifts! Watch out!" Ashleigh warned, but she was too late. Damian was hit square in the chest by one of the blasts, sending him falling toward the ground. Max nodded at Ashleigh, and she soared down after him while Max went to destroy the leading spaceship.

He rocketed up toward the largest spaceship of all, the leading one, and shot a blast of blue fire at it. It was completely unharmed and kept moving slowly toward NYC. "Fine. See how you like this!" Max growled. He drew a fireball on one of its wings and flew backward before it detonated. It blew up on the wing, making a hole right through it. Max flew to the other wing and did the same thing to it, making a large hole through it. The spaceship started to fall toward the city, gaining speed as it fell.

Ashleigh flew up beside Max, with Damian, Connor, and Jessica in tow. Max gestured toward the spaceship, conveying a silent message to the rest of the team. "Got it," they chorused.

Ashleigh flew to the front of the spaceship with Damian, Connor at the back of it with Jessica, and Max under it, right in the middle. They pushed and pulled with all their strength, but it was so large that their efforts were pointless. The spaceship started to fall again, and there was nothing they could do.

Then a pink figure flew past Max, and a glowing pink sphere appeared around the spaceship, keeping anything but the figure from getting to the spaceship. It turned around to face the group, and Max figured out that the "it" wasn't an it at all: a girl his age had stopped the airship from destroying the city. She increased the pressure on the spaceship and crushed it to the size of a paper ball. She threw it up into the sky and sliced it with a glowing magenta sword. The others flew toward the rest of the spaceships, destroying them as they flew.

Max threw a giant flame at a ship, setting it ablaze, while Connor and Ashleigh worked together to split other spacecrafts in half. They quickly destroyed all the ships, returning to the new girl.

"What's your name?" Max inquired, seizing the pause to ask.

"My name's Trina," she told him. "Yours?"

"Max," Max answered. Max noted that Trina had light-brown skin, with Afro-textured black hair that was packed into a puff. She wore a china-pink T-shirt with leggings of a matching color. All that clothing was covered with a slightly darker pink cloak. Trina held a glowing pink sword in her right hand, and it pulsed brightly as she studied the other kids.

"I'd assume we're going back down, right?" Trina asked. They all nodded in agreement. At that, Trina opened a portal, sending the group onto a street in their home city of Manhattan.

"Phew, we're back!" Max sighed in relief. Then he looked up and saw hundreds of aliens with photon blasters in one hand, laser swords in the other. They had jet packs on their backs and were heading straight toward the kids.

They landed on the ground, surrounding them. Their faces were light blue, but they looked pretty much like humans. Trina charged forward, attacking two aliens with one swing of her sword. They began firing their photon rays at the kids, but Damian created an ice dome around the group, blocking their blasts. Trina slashed an alien on the arm and kicked them backward, sending them sprawling on the ground. Trina then focused on her other opponent, slashing and swinging her sword at them.

The rest of the aliens moved toward Damian's ice dome, preparing their swords. They easily cut through the ice, exposing the five kids. Max, thinking on his feet, placed his palms on the ground, preparing to attack. Fire tendrils erupted out of the ground, entangling several aliens. Trina then cut through the incapacitated aliens with her sword, moving gracefully on the ground.

Then the remaining aliens took to the air, flying in the direction of a small cloud. Ashleigh and Jessica gave chase, thundering after them. Ashleigh called down a bolt of lightning on one of the aliens, and it struck them straight on the back. The alien went tumbling out of the sky, falling to their death. Jessica drew water from the ocean near her, shooting a giant bubble of water at the two aliens closest to her. The bubble encased them, and Jessica dropped them out of the air.

The remaining aliens flew over the small cloud, but Ashleigh and Jessica aimed to go through it, hoping to cut them off. But when they touched the cloud, they felt something cold and hard, like a...

Jessica pulled a giant, rushing stream of water from the ocean, shooting it at the object to clear out the cloud. The stream cleared, revealing another black alien ship. Jessica started, "Should we—"

"Yes," Ashleigh cut in. "I'll make a hole in there, and you flood it."

Jessica nodded. Ashleigh created a lightning dagger, plunging it into the ship. She then moved in a wide circle from that spot, cutting it off. Then when the shape was made, she kicked it off, creating a huge opening. "Now!" Ashleigh yelled. Jessica pulled another giant stream of water from the ocean, sending it straight into the hole. The ship rocked from side to side as the water sloshed around.

Inside the ship, the aliens buzzed around like honeybees that had lost their hive. "We need to get out of here!" one said. The others nodded, frantically moving toward an escape hatch at the back of the ship. One of them pulled a small device from their back, placing it on the hatch. The device beeped rapidly for a couple seconds, unlocking the hatch. They climbed out of the space, dropping out of the ship.

Jessica stopped channeling water into the ship, preparing to completely destroy it. She raised her arms, and the water raised with her. She spread her arms apart, and the water pushed on every side of the ship. Jessica knit her brows in concentration, trying to push the water out. The water heaved at the ship, slowly causing it to bulge. Then without warning, it forced itself out, breaking the ship from several ends. Ashleigh shot forward, cutting the pieces of the ship into even tinier pieces. Jessica then caught the debris in a giant water bubble, dropping it into the ocean when it was full.

"Our work here is done," Jessica said, wiping sweat off her brow.

Ashleigh nodded. "But the aliens we were chasing, where are they?" she asked. She looked down and answered her question. They had gone back down to fight everyone else! "We need to go help the others!" Ashleigh yelled, beginning to fly toward her friends. Jessica followed her, cracking her knuckles.

The moment Ashleigh's feet touched the ground, she punched an alien in the face, elbowing another in the gut. But she was caught off guard by a strike to the head from the blunt edge of a sword. She collapsed, going unconscious as Trina stabbed the alien that hit Ashleigh with her sword.

The aliens started to move toward Ashleigh, noticing that she was down. But Trina wasn't about to let that happen. She threw a ball of pink energy at the ground in front of the group of aliens, catching their attention. "Get Ashleigh out of the street," Trina said. "I'll deal with these extraterrestrials." Nodding, the kids picked Ashleigh up and scrambled out before the aliens could try and catch them, leaving Trina to fight them.

Trina flew up into the air with the aliens on her tail. Then she used a telekinetic pulse to push them away. While the aliens fell, she flew back down to the ground, preparing to attack with her sword. The aliens got back up, running at Trina and slicing at her with their swords. She countered most of them, but their strength was truly in numbers. Wanting to do as much damage as she could before they overwhelmed her, Trina flew into the air, absorbing her sword's energy.

Charging up the amount of energy she had left, Trina continued her ascent. *If they think I'm going down without a fight, they've never met us humans*, she thought with a grin. Pink rings of energy pulsed around Trina, and she flew faster for a few seconds. *Let's do this!* she thought, curving back down.

Trina flew faster, a conical white ring of air and water molecules formed around her as she broke the sound barrier. A loud *boom* could be heard as Trina rushed toward the ground. Pink energy surrounded her as air rushed through her hair. The aliens below her were confused as to what that pink thing flying toward them was, but they got into a defensive position, swords raised. *I can't be getting stabbed by a sword at this point, can I?* Trina thought. She crossed her arms and formed an *X* shape (sort of like the "Wakanda forever" thing), and a shield appeared in front of her.

The shield appeared right on time as she slammed into the ground not even a second after. The impact formed a crater in the ground, throwing several alien soldiers into buildings. Some of them had all their bones crushed into a powder at once, destroyed by Trina's power. But there were a few smart ones that stayed away, surviving the blow unscathed. Covering their eyes to shield them from the dust cloud that rose into the air, they walked forward, prepared to acquire Trina.

Trina managed to open her eyes and look up as the remaining alien soldiers picked her up. Summoning the remainder of her energy, Trina kicked an alien in the neck. Then she closed her eyes and fell unconscious. The alien soldiers grabbed her and flew into their only remaining spaceship, locking her inside a small electric containment chamber. They placed several special power-dampening crystals around the space, ensuring that Trina would stay down. Then they left her, leaving to attend to other matters.

* * * * *

Meanwhile, the other kids were in the ocean. Not the best idea, especially in the Atlantic, but as long as they had Jessica, they'd be fine. Jessica had created a water bubble around them so they could breathe, and they swam slowly for a few minutes—that is, until a frenzy of white-tipped sharks started circling around them.

The kids made no sudden moves and stayed completely still. Connor, though, moved backward and tripped over Ashleigh, waking her up.

Meanwhile, the sharks had stopped circling and were all staring at the water bubble, poised to strike. "Is this a bad thing?" Connor asked.

"Probably, but I think Jessica will take care of it," Damian said.

"Okay," Connor said.

The sharks waited…waited…and waited for what felt like years—and then they struck! They bit down so fast Jessica didn't have time to react. The bubble popped and exposed the other four, which was really bad, considering that Jessica's friends couldn't breathe underwater like she could. But they all knew how to swim, at least.

The kids swam for dear life, and Jessica boosted them with water (what else are friends for?). They escaped to the land, leaving Jessica to fend off the sharks. For a while, Jessica tried to outswim them, but they were coming at her from all directions. Then she thought, *OMG, I'm in water!* She spun around and created some sort of whirlpool, disorienting the sharks and saving her life. She flew out of the ocean and met Connor on his surfboard, where he was hovering two feet above the water.

"Finally! Took you long enough," Connor exclaimed.

"I was defending myself from sharks, not playing beach volleyball!" Jessica returned.

Connor rolled his eyes, saying, "Guess what."

"What?" Jessica pressed.

"Trina's been taken by the aliens."

"What! How?"

"How am I supposed to know?"

"We need to find her—fast," Jessica said. If anything, she wasn't about to let a teammate get abducted. She remembered something that Damian had done when they were fighting one of the past villains. He had been able to create a giant war avatar, so Jessica obviously did the same thing. Naturally, her avatar was dark blue, but it was equipped with a whip and a pair of giant wings. She was safe inside the head of her avatar. Connor stared at her in wide-eyed amazement as her avatar flew into the air.

"What? We have a teammate to save," Jessica said.

Connor and Jessica silently flew through the clouds for several minutes before she asked, "Wait, do you even know where we're going?"

Connor nearly fell off his flying surfboard before saying, "Yes."

"How?" Jessica asked. "If you already knew where Trina was, why didn't you go get her with the rest of the team?"

"Because I didn't necessarily know where she was. I just have a sense of her energy."

"Hmmm, 'cause that's normal."

"And your powers are?"

Jessica rolled her eyes. "So how did you acquire this sense of energy?"

"Well, that's because I'm an alien," Connor said.

"What!" Jessica yelled, backing up.

"The good kind!" Connor quickly clarified, mentally berating himself for phrasing it terribly.

"Yeah, makes sense, considering the fact that we found you in an ice cube!" Jessica half-yelled.

Connor cringed.

"You know what? I'll yell at you later. We have a teammate to save," Jessica said, moving forward.

Connor followed, wanting to help his teammate as well.

The pair then reached an oddly shaped cloud, and Connor stopped. "Here," he said. He got off his flying surfboard and stood on top of the cloud. He felt around on the cloud until he felt a latch, and he opened it. "C'mon, in!" he whispered.

Jessica shrank her avatar just enough to fit inside the hatch, and the pair jumped inside and looked around, finding the control system unguarded.

They couldn't understand the different symbols and signs, so they simply clicked random buttons and then hid. As an alien soldier walked past, the two decided to rescue Trina and get out, but that was easier said than done. The soldier moved to the control pad and frowned, seeing that several things had been tampered with. Connor and Jessica left, using the soldier's distraction to their advantage. They roamed long dark passageways for minutes, avoiding alien soldiers, until finally they found Trina.

CHAPTER 8

Aliens Have a Planet—Wow, Just Wow

They had finally found her. They had found Trina! Although there was a minor problem: sentries. About six of them were guarding Trina's cell and saw the kids coming before they even reached them. A sentry pulled a small device out of their pocket and threw it at Jessica. Jessica quickly created a ball of water, surrounding the device with it. But then, right as she was about to let out a sigh of relief, the device beeped. "What!" Jessica shouted right as the device exploded.

Water and steam shot in every direction, and both the sentries and the kids ducked. But Jessica had a plan. She spun the steam into a small cloud, creating a thick cover to block the sentries' view. "Quick!" Jessica hissed to Connor.

The two launched themselves forward, taking advantage of the cover. "You free Trina, and I'll deal with the sentries," Jessica said, and Connor nodded. Connor focused on the cell holding Trina, feeling around for the lock. His hands moved around blindly until he felt a little depression in the cell. He stuck his pinkie into the space and felt around, trying to get the shape of the lock. Then with his other hand, he created a rock key to fit into the lock, thinking, *Yes!*

As Connor did that, Jessica used her avatar's fists to pummel the sentries around her. The mist cover was fading away due to the movement in the space, but it had given the kids a small advantage.

Jessica kicked a sentry in the jaw, elbowing another in the ribs. The bodies of sentries flew into the air around her, kicked around like rag dolls. Almost all the sentries had been dealt with. Except for one. "Wanna dance?" Jessica asked calmly.

The male sentry grinned and unsheathed his laser sword, charging at Jessica. Jessica quickly created a water whip and wrapped it around the sentry, restraining him. But then the sentry took his sword and sliced through the end of the whip holding him, freeing himself. *He's a slippery one*, Jessica thought.

Jessica moved forward and placed her hands on the ground, creating a giant wave of water. It rushed toward the sentry, roaring as it moved. The sentry grinned, rubbing his palms together. An orange glowing ball of fire grew in between his hands, getting larger by the moment. *He has the same power as Max?* Jessica thought in confusion.

After a couple seconds, the fireball was several feet in height, width, and depth, and the sentry was about to throw it. He jumped into the air to dodge the water wave and twisted around, launching it straight at Jessica.

Jessica grinned, increasing the height of her avatar by two feet. Then she raised the water wave in front of her, ready to block the fireball. The flames slammed into the water wall, steam rising into the air. A hissing sound could be heard as the two elements collided. Jessica outstretched her arms, trying to hold the water wave up as the fireball ate away at it.

Connor led Trina out of her cell, fully aware of Jessica's situation. Through the corner of his eye, he spotted the sentry, focusing the fire at the water wall. Connor outstretched his arms, and four vines shot out of them. They wrapped themselves around the sentry while another vine yanked the laser sword away from him and threw it into the air. "Trina!" Connor called.

Trina rushed forward, grabbing the laser sword. She pulled her arm back and swung at the sentry. His eyes widened in fear, and he started to struggle and yell in the vines, but to no avail. It was over in a matter of seconds. The water wave disappeared, and Jessica's avatar faded away. "Glad to know *you're* in good shape," she said to Trina.

Trina winked, forming an *X* shape with her arms. "Stay behind me, and you won't be hurt."

Connor and Jessica moved directly behind Trina, preparing for whatever she was about to do. Trina charged her energy, flexing her invisible muscles. A powerful rush of air swirled around her, blowing away anything within a four-foot radius. Connor shielded himself and Jessica from the wind with a rock wall, thinking, *Such raw power!*

Trina then forced her arms apart, pushing the air away from her and adding her own energy to it. Any and everything in front or beside her was obliterated, but Jessica and Connor were safe. As the ship was destroyed, Trina teleported herself and the other two away, cloak flying.

The kids appeared on a sidewalk somewhere in central New York, but Trina fell to her knees, gasping.

"Are you okay?" Jessica asked, rushing to her side. Trina shook her head. Connor, a memory clicking in his head, moved Trina's cloak out of the way, looking at her arms. He searched her left arm but found nothing unusual. Then he took a look at her right arm, and there, right above the crease in her arm, lay a red glowing *N*.

"Trina has the mark of Ne'faro," Connor said, head spinning.

"What's the mark of Ne'faro?" Jessica asked.

"It's a symbol that drains the energy of the carrier and gives it to the brander, also killing the carrier after forty-eight hours," Connor answered meekly.

"What!" Jessica screamed. "Is there a cure?" she asked.

"Yes, on the planet Naturae-37," Connor answered.

"Makes enough sense, given the fact that you're an alien," Jessica muttered to herself. "Let's go."

Connor lifted the now unconscious Trina, floating into the air. Jessica floated after him, charging her energy for the trip. "But wait!" she exclaimed as she remembered their team. "We need to get the rest of the crew first."

"Okay, you do that while I take Trina to Naturae-37," Connor replied.

"All right then," Jessica said as she flew away. "Alexa, call Ashleigh."

In no time, Jessica was speaking with Ashleigh on her smart earbud. Ashleigh relayed to Jessica that she and the two other boys were at the Empire State Building, hovering on top of it.

In three minutes, the kids were passing the thermosphere, although it was extremely hot. They breezed through the exosphere, and Jessica thought it would be like the thermosphere, but the heat was more bearable.

Finally they made it into outer space and were bathed in the sun's rays. They glimpsed Connor and Trina nearing a constellation that looked like a panther, Jessica already naming it. *Stella Panthera*, she thought.

The kids followed them into the middle of Stella Panthera and saw a glowing green planet. Jessica took one good look at it and knew that it was Naturae-37. They entered its cool atmosphere, rocketing toward the lush green ground. The kids landed on the green grass and were soon surrounded by alien people.

The aliens' eyes were glowing green, and they had their arms outstretched, ready to fight. "Do not move," an elder said.

The kids raised their hands up in surrender, but one of the alien kids exclaimed, "It's Connor! The champion has returned!" This caused them to all stare at him.

An elder stepped forward. "Connor Nightingale, please come forth," he ordered. Connor stepped out from behind Jessica and moved to the middle of the circle.

"You have been gone for three years, and now you just come waltzing back in like nothing ever happened," an old woman growled, extending a finger.

"Then you shouldn't have given me that last quest," Connor snapped, biting back at her. "I was frozen in ice for three years before these kind humans rescued me. You didn't even bother to check on me through your looking glass!" he yelled.

"She has a *looking glass*!" Damian asked, covering his mouth. "That is *hilarious*!" He giggled, bursting into laughter.

The old woman looked taken aback, but she quickly regained her old composure.

Jessica whispered to Damian, "And so is the fact that aliens have a planet."

"I should have you sent to the mines for that act of insolence," she snapped, pointing at Damian.

Well boo-hoo, Jessica and Damian thought in unison, glancing at each other.

"Also, I have been watching your pett—" the old woman started.

"Do you know when to quit? 'Cause I can teach you," Connor offered.

"Oh, please. You have enough nerve to interrupt me, yet you can't even beat me in a duel!" She laughed.

Oh my God, stop! Damian and Jessica thought, covering their mouths to stop themselves from laughing.

"I've learned much, Gwendolyn," Connor warned. When the old grandma wouldn't back down, Connor sighed, then slammed his fists on the grass, sending a huge crack running through the ground straight at Gwendolyn. She disappeared in a burst of purple smoke, reappearing behind Connor.

The circle of people grew sparse as the people began to run away, pointing at the skies and screaming. Connor's eyes widened as he remembered why they came here in the first place and when he saw what his people were screaming about.

"What were you thinking!" Jessica yelled.

"It's time to get the crystal!" he yelled back through the commotion. He continued to stare at the sky.

"What are you doi—"

"Shh! Look!" He pointed at a giant, planet-eating, lava-spitting mechanical snake.

Jessica's jaw dropped to the ground when she saw the machine. "We need to get the crystal now," she said, already motioning for Connor to get a move on.

"Agreed."

They ran through the crowd, with Connor in the lead. They dug down into the ground and saw many different glowing crystals. Then they found an off-limits section, which, of course, they violated. When they walked in, there was only one crystal. It was aqua green and shiny. "This is called the Crystal of Ne'cura," Connor explained.

"So we need to take some back to Trina," Jessica responded.

Connor nodded.

"Okay." Jessica broke off a small piece that was as big as two nickels. "All right, let's go," Jessica ordered, already flying out.

"Wait for me!" Connor yelled.

They flew out to see total and utter destruction. The once-green ground was now scorched and black. The people were gone, and alien troops from the mechanical snake were now carrying out crystals from holes to the core of the planet. "We've got to stop them!" Connor cried as he ran toward the troops.

"Stop!" Jessica yelled as she yanked his arm back. She pointed to Trina, who was still lying unconscious a mere twenty feet away. Jessica took the crystal and ran over to Trina.

Jessica was about to force-feed her when Connor yelled, "Wait, you need to put the crystal on the mark."

"Oh!"

"Yeah, now lemme have it."

"Okay."

Connor took the crystal and put it on Trina's mark. The red mark pulsated before disappearing into the crystal. Connor threw the crystal on the ground, shattering it. "What did you do!" Jessica yelled frantically.

"The crystal will get absorbed back into the ground. Just watch," Connor clarified.

The shattered crystal dissolved into the ground, and Trina stirred. She finally came to and got up, making her pink cloak billow.

"All right, this is weird. I have a couple questions for you guys, if you don't mind. Where are we, what are you doing, and lastly, where are the others?" Trina asked.

"We are on the planet Naturae-37, we just saved your life, and I don't know," Jessica said.

Trina's mouth made a perfect *O*, and she stared at something behind Jessica.

"There's an evil alien soldier that's preparing to kill me, isn't there?" Jessica figured.

Trina nodded.

Shoot.

Connor raised the ground behind Jessica and sent the alien soldier flying. Perfect!

"Trina, how much energy do you have?" Connor asked.

"I'm almost fully charged," Trina said, making Jessica think she was a robot and not a human.

"Could you send us to the core?" Connor inquired.

Trina hovered in the air and teleported them to the core with a flash. "You're welcome," Trina said.

"Oh, *thanks*," Jessica replied.

"Yep. I'm here all week."

"Next time I need you, I'll call."

"Here's my business card."

Ignoring the girls' playful banter, Connor found the core untouched, thankfully. What he saw behind them was a completely different matter. They found the old woman creeping up on Connor (the nerve of this crone was outrageous). "What do you want now?" Connor sighed. "Did you come for a rematch?" He smirked.

Trina laughed. Gwendolyn blew a cloud of purple smoke toward them, but Trina created a portal and sent it away. The crone shamelessly threw a ball of energy at Trina, who deflected it with her sword. "If you're gonna throw balls of energy at me, I might as well tell you that this sword is made of raw telekinetic energy, so you might want to quit now," Trina said, twirling her sword.

Gwendolyn seemed to ponder over the idea of being vaporized by a telekinetic sword. She glared at Trina icily, screaming, "I will have my *revenge!*" as she disappeared in a cloud of purple smoke.

"Man, if looks could kill, that glare would have vaporized me," Trina joked.

"Mm-hmm," Jessica agreed. Anyway, she noted that the core of the planet was only as big as a pack of twelve cookies from Super Savers.

"We need to take the core and replace it with something hot that's the same size," Connor said.

"How about Max's fire?" Jessica asked.

"That could work," he agreed, nodding.

Jessica looked at Trina. She immediately used her telepathy to find Max. They had very little time to take the core, and it was running out.

As this happened, the other kids were trapped in a cell like animals. They had tried breaking the bars with their powers, but nothing worked.

"These bars are made of titanium crystals," an alien soldier said.

"Thanks, but *I'd* like to know how you can even *speak* English," Ashleigh snapped.

"You better be quiet. Don't forget that we're in an *alien* warship, not our own warship. Also, you need a Snickers," Damian whispered.

"What he said," Max agreed.

"Shut up." Ashleigh groaned.

Suddenly Max felt a sharp pain in his head. A voice called, *Max, Max, where are you?*

Max answered in his mind, *In the warship.*

The voice asked another question, *Where are the others?*

With me in a cell, Max replied.

Okay, thanks, the voice said.

The pulsing in Max's head stopped. The voice was gone.

"Max, are you okay?" Ashleigh asked.

"Yeah," he said. Suddenly he saw a flash of dark pink, blue, and green.

Trina, Jessica, and Connor had come to get them out. "It's about time," Ashleigh muttered under her breath.

"Drama queen," Damian retorted quietly.

Trina slashed the crystalline material with her sword, and the bars broke. "Quick, before the alien scouts see us," Trina cautioned. They raced out of the chamber and were about to jump out when an alien soldier stopped them.

The soldier was about a foot taller than Max and had many weapons. The soldier had one plasma ray, a sword, a mini-target rocket launcher, and sonic bombs.

"I hope he's a friendly one," Ashleigh whispered.

"Me too," Max replied.

"Wait, how do you know it's a he?" Damian asked.

Max shrugged, signaling Damian to discontinue the subject.

The soldier unsheathed his sword. "Die!" he yelled.

He charged at the kids with his sword in his right hand. Max ducked under his swing, analyzing the situation. Trina cut out a big oval in the ship and yelled at the others to jump out before the soldier swung again.

"Darn, that's a long way down," Ashleigh worried. She squealed but jumped. So did everyone else. The soldier stayed on his warcraft and stared down, not needing or wanting to follow them. He wasn't ever going to get them.

CHAPTER 9

Catch That War Machine!

They were falling. Falling through the sky, rockets of peace and hope. Trina just *had* to spoil it by creating a portal. Straight to the center of Naturae-37. The kids landed on dirt, and Ashleigh had to get up and dust herself off. It was *horrible*, she thought.

"Max, come here!" Trina called. Max ran over to Trina, and they babbled on about weight, size, heat, and all that boring science stuff. When they were done, Max created a ball of fire that was as big as a pack of Super Savers cookies. Trina contained the core in a telekinetic ball, and Max put his fire in place of the core. The planet shook for a second, dropping a little dirt, but it quickly stopped.

"That was—"

"Don't!" Ashleigh cut Max off, knowing what he was going to say next.

"Easy," Max finished.

Ashleigh face-palmed. "You idiot, you just jinxed us!" She was proven right as a troop of soldiers flooded the chamber and raised their weapons.

There were about fifty of them, and twenty of them held crystal bows with poison tipped arrows nocked. Another five of them had plasma rays, and five more wielded glowing laser swords. The rest held white spherical objects that looked suspiciously like bombs. An alien commander walked through the troops and said in perfect

English, "We don't want to hurt you children. Hand over the core, and we'll be going away."

"Wash off the blue dye on your face, and I'll probably trust you," Ashleigh said calmly. The aliens' faces darkened, and Connor hissed.

"Do not insult us! You are powerless children and shouldn't be trying to fight something you have no control over. Give me the core!" the commander yelled.

The kids stood side to side, drawing upon their elemental powers. A flame danced in the air, a stream of water curling around the kids. Sparks flew above the commander's head, and an icy wind chilled the air. Two pink glowing swords appeared in Trina's hands, and the earth rumbled as Connor spoke.

"When you said we were powerless children, were you being literal or metaphorical?"

The commander gritted his teeth, saying, "You leave us no choice. Troops, attack."

The archers jumped onto the sides of the chamber. They stuck to the rocks and nocked their arrows, firing moments later. Three arrows hurtled through the air toward Ashleigh. Max threw a giant ball of fire at the arrows, but they absorbed the flames, glowing dark orange. The arrows still flew through the air at Ashleigh, but she rolled out of the way just a millisecond before they struck the ground. The arrows promptly burst into flame. Damian threw a slab of ice at one of the archers, hitting the soldier's shoulder and making the alien drop their weapon.

"Duck!" Max yelled to Ashleigh as an arrow zipped through the air. She ducked and felt a rush of air from the arrow. Moving away, she zipped toward the group of aliens with bombs. She sent a bolt of lightning at one bomb, hoping to set it off in the wielder's face. Sadly, alien technology didn't work that way. The aliens launched several bombs at Ashleigh, and she hit them all with electricity, but they absorbed her attack, just like the arrows! The bombs stopped in midair and formed a circle around Ashleigh: one above her head, one at each of her sides, and two at her feet. They turned into discs and started blasting out high-frequency sound.

Ashleigh's eardrums felt like they were going to pop out of her ears at any time. She was brought to her knees by the piercing sound of the discs, and her vision was getting blurry. The sound increased, and she doubled over and landed flat on her face as consciousness faded away.

Through the corner of her eye, Jessica noticed Ashleigh drop to the ground. *I need to help her*, Jessica thought, wrapping her water whip around an alien's neck. *But I'm occupied with these stupid aliens!* She yanked the water whip, cutting off all air to the alien and effectively killing them. *Never mind.* She rushed to Ashleigh's side, placing her hands on the ground. Two giant waves of water pushed the sonic disks out and washed the soldiers surrounding her away. Jessica then picked Ashleigh up and scurried back to the rest of the group.

"Great, Ashleigh's out cold." Max sighed as he saw Jessica.

"Oh, good job! When did you figure it out?" Jessica said sarcastically.

Max said nothing as he threw a fireball at an alien.

Meanwhile, Trina was cornered in a swords-to-swords fight with three of the soldiers. Trina wielded two while each soldier only wielded one. She spun and twirled, parrying and striking at the soldiers. All three soldiers glanced at each other and nodded, spreading around Trina. They then swung at Trina's head at the same time, hoping to finally get rid of her. But Trina was quick and ducked right before the swords hit her. She then stuck one of her energy swords through a soldier's chest, twisting it around as his insides sizzled.

Trina then moved to make quick work of the remaining soldiers but was surprised when Jessica lassoed the two. She threw them into another soldier that was fighting Damian and Max, causing groans of pain to erupt from the aliens' mouths.

"Remind me to never get in the way of Jessica's rage," Max muttered.

"Agreed," Damian said, nodding.

"Shut up and *fight!*" Jessica screamed as she lassoed another alien.

"Savage," Damian whispered to Max as he froze an alien.

Max kicked another alien in the stomach and whispered, "Ooh, that kick is gonna hurt him for days!"

"Yep. Jessica's cringing already," Damian replied, motioning his head toward Jessica.

Max spun around and set himself on fire, disappearing and reappearing behind an alien. "When did you master that technique!" Jessica asked in amazement.

"While Ashleigh, Damian, and I were trapped in that prison in the alien *Warsnake*, I created it," Max explained as he torched the last sword alien.

"Heads up—archer!" Damian warned Jessica. She looked up to see an alien aiming an arrow at her from the stone "ceiling." Damian tackled her to the ground, and they spun, barely dodging the arrow as it cut through the air. Damian rolled off Jessica and to his feet, striking the archer in the gut with an icicle.

Max appeared next to Ashleigh, torching a sword-wielding alien that had crept up on her as she stirred. Ashleigh blinked twice, trying to understand her surroundings. Then an archer fired at her and she rolled backward, remembering everything that had occurred in the past few minutes.

"Glad to see *you're* alive and kickin'," Max said, twisting around to dodge an arrow.

"When you're in the middle of a fight with soldiers and half your team use only one-fourth of their brain, *someone* has to work," Ashleigh wittily replied.

Max rolled his eyes, going back to back with Ashleigh. Ashleigh focused a beam of electricity on an alien, and they crumpled to the ground. Max then ran forward and, with half the strength in his arms, slammed his fist into an alien's stomach. The alien was sent flying into the wall, creating a small crater. Another alien with a sword rushed at the two, but they were prepared.

"Dagger," Max said, and Ashleigh nodded.

Ashleigh formed a lightning dagger, and Max created a fire blade. The two moved forward, unfazed by the laser sword of the alien. The alien swung in a wide arc, but the duo ducked, evading the attack. Ashleigh then moved behind the alien, taking their right side.

Max took the left, clutching his dagger tightly. The two lunged forward and thrust their daggers through the alien. Now it was down to only one alien soldier. Ashleigh turned around and kicked the alien into the air, and Max jumped up and pressed his hand to the alien's face. An orange glowing palm print appeared on his face, glowing brighter as the moments passed. Right as the alien hit the ground, the mark exploded, defeating them.

The others looked on in wonder at the pair's teamwork. Max turned around, revealing the core. "I have the core. Let's get out of here."

Trina created a large portal, and the kids hopped in, reappearing on the lush green grass of Naturae-37. Max decided to take a look around, simply to survey the land. He then flew away. "So what do we do now?" Trina asked.

The kids began to converse on what they should do next, what with getting the core.

"I'm just gonna listen to some music," Ashleigh said, not wanting to waste her breath on the topic. "Alexa," she continued, "play me my summer playlist."

"Don't tell me you have a *specific* playlist for the summer!" Damian gasped exasperatedly.

"Any problems?" Ashleigh asked, annoyed. Damian glared at her, but he kept his mouth shut (thankfully).

Jessica rolled her eyes at the pair's antics. She expelled water from her body in a pulse, knocking Damian down and filling Ashleigh's mouth with water. Trina teleported away so she wasn't affected. Ashleigh gushed water out of her mouth like a water fountain.

Suddenly Connor appeared next to Jessica. "I'm here, guys!" he said enthusiastically.

"Great! You can explain to us what to do next," Jessica said. Before Connor could respond, Max returned to tell them that he'd scouted ahead and had found fifty three-gallon tanks of plasma being loaded into the *Warsnake*. Connor gaped at him like a fish.

"And you did nothing about it!" he asked, bewildered.

"Uh…"

"Do you know how many people could be *killed* with 150 gallons of plasma!"

"No, but I have a good estimate. Over seven thousand aliens and/or people could be…" *I'm hating myself more and more with every syllable,* Max realized.

"Mm-hmm," Connor agreed. With that, Connor jumped hundreds of feet into the air and flew off to find the *Warsnake.*

"Isn't he being…you know, reckless?" Jessica asked calmly.

"What do you *think*?" Max replied as he pyro-ported away.

Ashleigh turned into a bolt of electricity with a sigh. Damian spun around and turned into a blizzard, flying around like it was Christmas. Trina created a portal and waved bye before stepping in and disappearing inside it. And then there was one. Jessica was the only *normal* person, so she flew. She caught up with Connor and spotted one last tank of plasma as it was being loaded into the *Warsnake* down below.

Connor instantly threw himself into a nosedive, aiming straight for the center of the *Warsnake.* Connor created boulders and hurled them at the *Warsnake*, but they just bounced off the alien metal. "Shoot," Connor muttered. He flew back up into the sky and disappeared inside the bright-green clouds.

Suddenly a bolt of electricity struck the *Warsnake*, coursing through the alien metal and setting its tail on fire. The bolt turned into Ashleigh, who asked, "Need help?"

"Yep," Jessica said.

Ashleigh nodded and threw bolts of electricity at the *Warsnake*, making multiple things on its tail explode. Without warning, the *'Snake* shuddered, and its tail grew back!

"Um, Connor, *help!*" Jessica yelled.

Connor raised the ground below the *'Snake* and formed a giant hand out of rocks. The hand grabbed the Snake right in the middle of its metal body and held it in place. But the *Warsnake* must really have been made for conquest because it secreted lava through chinks in its metal armor. The rocks melted and flowed down onto the ground, allowing the *Warsnake* to fly off.

Connor appeared next to Jessica, shaking his head in disbelief as he said, "If that *'Snake* just took out the hardest rocks in the galaxy, think about what it could do to *planets*."

"I know, right?" Ashleigh agreed.

Max appeared next to Jessica, eyes blazing (literally) as he added, "Connor, what were you *thinking* going off like that? No offense, but what did you accomplish by yourself? We just need to work *together* to destroy the *Warsnake*. We can't just split up and leave one another behind. We're a team. Teams work together, and so should we. Now off that subject, that *'Snake* isn't gonna get away. *Catch that war machine!*" With those words of empowerment, they all darted off after the *Warsnake*.

Have you ever turned into a bolt of electricity? Oh, and turned into electricity while you're moving super-duper-fast? Well, if you have, you know that it hurts. At least the pain is masked by the feeling of air rushing through your hair.

Anyway, the kids flew after the *Warsnake* and almost caught it, but it opened all of its scales/flap thingies and flew around in spirals, spraying lava everywhere! Max was disoriented and dropped the core. Two metal hands came out from the *'Snake*'s tail, grabbing the core into the *'Snake*.

"Well, shoot," Ashleigh said.

"We've lost," Trina said softly, though matter-of-factly.

"No, we can't lose," Max said firmly. "Did the Avengers stop when Ultron almost decimated them? No! So should we stop just because we lost one of the most powerful objects in the universe? Absolutely not!"

"Max is right. We can't give up," Connor agreed.

Max disappeared in a ball of fire, and the only thing left of him was black smoke that didn't rise. Ignoring the fact that Max had referenced a movie that had been made seventy-three years ago, the kids followed.

They chased the *Warsnake* for another twenty million miles— that is, until they settled on a fiery planet that the *'Snake* landed on. It drilled down into the ground, surprising a few natives of the planet. Max glanced at a few of them, realization dawning on him.

"Guys, these are fire aliens! You guys go after the 'Snake. I'll talk to them."

Connor nodded in approval, earning a rude comment from Damian. "Who made *you* the team leader?" he muttered. Connor ignored him and jumped into the hole, followed by the others.

An elder approached, saying, "A duel?"

Max nodded (though finding it a bit weird), and with a snap of his fingers, the ground around them, which was made of obsidian, formed into a circle. The elder outstretched his arms and sent a wave of blue fire toward Max.

Max easily evaded it and returned his own beam of fire at the elder. The elder jumped into the sky and aimed a kick at Max, but just when he got close, Max grabbed his leg and swung him back into the air. Max jumped and kicked the elder with both feet, sending him flying out of the circle.

An alien child walked up to her mother, who was watching the match, and exclaimed, "Mommy, Father is back!" Her mother looked at her, surprised, but then studied Max a bit more.

She muttered sentences such as, "Hmmm, he has the same hair color," and "Same combat skills too." Finally she seemed to be satisfied and said, "Yes, it's true, the warrior's aura emanates from his soul. But he isn't Ragnar."

The elder walked back, rubbing his temple. "How did this happen?" he pondered.

"I felt the pulse of the crystal. He was defeated in battle," the woman confirmed.

"But why did he choose a child like you?" the elder asked.

"I have no idea, but I'll do my best to protect this planet," Max said, thinking, *What the heck is going on?*

The elder chuckled. "He has the bravery of our warrior too."

Max flushed red but held his head up. *Why me??* He was about to leave when the elder handed an orange dye bottle to him. Max looked at him, and the elder just mouthed the words, "Take it. We will meet again." Max nodded and was about to jump into the hole when he remembered something.

"Wait!" he called to the elder.

The others chased the 'Snake through a long and winding maze created by none other than the 'Snake. They were gaining, but then Damian spotted a shadow not coming from any of them. It crawled on the walls and jumped onto him! Yes, shadows aren't physical manifestations, but this shadow was a *completely* different case. The shadow seeped into Damian's skin, like sunlight to a sunflower. He could feel himself being taken over.

Okay, this was getting ridiculous. Why Damian? The "shadow" could have picked Ashleigh, Jessica, Connor, maybe even Trina! So why him? Why? Anyway, Damian could feel his mind being sent on a permanent vacation, taking all his common sense with it.

Great. Now Damian had an excuse to act stupid. His irises frosted over (literally), and he could have sworn that the air temperature dropped by thirty degrees Fahrenheit.

"Man, it's getting chilly in here," Trina said as she tried to pull her cloak around herself.

"You can say that again," Jessica agreed. The temperature dropped by another fifteen degrees.

"Yep," Ashleigh said. "But wasn't it just sixty degrees or something?"

"You're right," Trina confirmed.

"Then why did the temperature…?" Ashleigh inquired.

"I don't know how it dropped by forty-five degrees, but something weird is going on," Trina said.

Suddenly Damian's mind went blank, and his body convulsed. He battled the power of the shadow, but he was losing rapidly. It was like his mind soldiers had straws to protect themselves, and the enemy had swords. "G-guys! St-stay back!" he stuttered as he tried to pull out the shadow. His attempts were futile as shadows aren't physical manifestations. Then again, at least he had an excuse for behaving stupidly.

Where's Athena when you need her? Damian heard a booming voice in his mind: *Speak.* He opened his mouth, but instead of his regular medium-pitched voice, he spoke with a deep voice and the sound of a couple hundred people: "Forget your quest, and I will spare you. Stop hunting down my cargo ship."

The girls stopped, confused, but Connor continued after the *'Snake*. "Damian!" Trina and Jessica exclaimed in unison. Jessica hovered over to help her teammate while Trina entered Damian's mind. But the shadow wanted otherwise. Damian subconsciously put up mental shields and forced Trina out of his brain. Then the shadow controlled his voice box *again*. "Get away from me!" he hissed coldly. The girls were taken by surprise, to say the least. Damian's body went cold. He had lost his mental battle. The shadow took full control over his body, and he attacked his friends.

CHAPTER 10

Spandex Is Back, Baby!

Damian attacked the girls, a blank expression on his face. He out-stretched both arms and shot separate beams of ice at the three. Jessica quickly leapt over one, spinning in the air as her hair flew. Trina quickly created a glowing shield in front of her, and the ice hissed as it hit. Ashleigh threw a bolt of lightning at the ice, canceling it out with a spark. The three girls slowly circled around Damian waiting for him to move. But Trina was already a step ahead. She peered into Damian's mind, trying to read his thoughts. But Damian wasn't in there. A dark, sinister entity curled around in his mind, controlling Damian. It snapped at Trina, and she quickly pulled out of Damian's mind, taking a step back. Whatever was causing him to do this was clearly sentient.

All of a sudden, Damian spun around, shooting icicles in every direction. Trina was the first to respond, creating a pink dome around Damian. The icicles didn't get far, hitting the dome before they could harm anyone.

"Thanks, Trina," Ashleigh and Jessica chorused.

Trina nodded, right as Damian created two ice swords. He thrust the two of them into the dome, cutting a small hole in it. *He isn't joking around, is he?* Trina thought as she created two swords of her own.

"Don't hurt him," Jessica said. "He's not in control of his body."

Trina scoffed. "That's like telling me not to hurt a tiger that's trying to attack me. I'm gonna die otherwise!"

Damian widened the hole in the dome, opening it up just enough for him to get through.

Trina moved about ten meters back, wanting to put some space between the two of them. *Don't interfere or he won't show mercy on you girls either,* Trina relayed to Jessica and Ashleigh. The two nodded, staying out of the way.

Damian took a step forward, his swords at his sides. He took another step. It was so quiet you could hear his footsteps bouncing around the tunnel. He took a third step, increasing his pace. Trina didn't move, analyzing her opponent. *Step, step, step, step.* Damian broke out into a run, dashing at Trina. But she held her ground. *Does she want to get herself killed?* Jessica and Ashleigh wondered. Their eyes locked, and they both wondered if they should interfere. *But Trina would have a plan. I know she wouldn't just die like that,* Ashleigh thought. She shook her head at Jessica, discouraging her from moving to stop Damian.

Now Damian was only five meters away from Trina. As he moved closer, Trina tilted her head down, a smirk bringing up a corner of her mouth. Damian raised one of his swords up, preparing to swing. Damian brought the sword down, letting it soar through the air straight at Trina. Then Trina moved. Quick as a flash, she used the flat side of her sword to block the hit. The sound of the two objects clashing echoed through the tunnel, piercing through the silence. Damian then brought his other sword arcing toward Trina's stomach. Alarmed, Trina teleported behind Damian, kicking him to the ground.

Damian fell with the combined weight of the swing *and* the kick, dirt getting into his mouth. He rolled to his feet, though, more enraged than he had already been. He threw both swords into the air, splitting them up into hundreds of tinier blades. Trina didn't raise her eyebrows, preparing to block the attack. Damian fired the tiny daggers, but not at Trina. No. The blades were aimed at the other two: Ashleigh and Jessica.

Trina's eyes widened, and she outstretched her arms to try to help. *I need a shield or something*, she thought. *Anything! I just need to stop those blades.* Trina forced some of her energy out of her, hoping desperately that it would do *something*. Then miraculously, time stopped.

Trina gazed at her surroundings as they were, frozen. *Did I do that?* Trina wondered in disbelief. She took a step forward, wondering if she could move. The answer was yes, and she put a foot forward. She then moved in front of Jessica and, with a powerful display of energy, pushed the blades away. She then teleported in front of Ashleigh and repeated the process. Now that the blades were gone, though, how was she going to resume time?

Well, pausing and resuming are opposites, Trina thought. *So if I pushed energy out to stop time, maybe pulling energy in would resume it.* Trina decided to test her theory and pulled all her energy back to her. At first, nothing happened, but then slowly, everything began to move again. Jessica pulled her arms away from her face as she realized that the blades were no longer in the air but rather on the ground, harmless. *What just happened?* she wondered. *I didn't see anything grab them out of the air, and I didn't blink either. So what?*

Trina rushed forward and tackled Damian, pinning him down. On Trina's thought, pink glowing chains shot out of the ground, wrapping around him. Jessica and Ashleigh moved to Trina's side, kneeling beside her. Trina placed her hands on Damian's head and closed her eyes as the other two girls placed their hands on her shoulders.

Trina reentered Damian's mind and looked around. Two figures appeared next to her: Jessica and Ashleigh. Ignoring the need to know how they'd followed her, she spotted the swirling black serpent that controlled her teammate. Trina unsheathed her sword, running toward the thing. Ashleigh and Jessica formed weapons of their own, running beside their friend. The serpent turned on them, revealing several sharp teeth and wings. But when it left whatever it was swirling around to fight the girls, it revealed a boy their age with black hair and a witty comment for everything: Damian. Damian made eye contact with Trina and formed a bow and arrow, putting a finger to his lips.

Trina nodded, engaging the serpent in combat. Ashleigh focused a beam of lightning on the serpent, making it recoil in surprise and pain. Jessica wrapped her whip around its neck, pulling hard. Trina jumped into the air, raising her sword. *This isn't going to be big enough,* she thought, increasing the size of her sword. She plunged the blade into the serpent's head, making it writhe in agony. All the while it shook its head, trying to fling Trina off, but she held tight.

Now Damian, behind the serpent, nocked an arrow and fired at the serpent's midsection. The arrow flew true, piercing the black mass. Right at that spot, a layer of ice spread, covering that part of the serpent. Noticing this, Damian fired a volley of arrows, keeping them going relentlessly. *Boom, boom, boom, boom,* the arrows hit their marks, freezing parts of the mass. Damian then nocked a giant arrow, aiming at the beast's head. He let the arrow fly, running forward to ensure that nothing would prevent it from hitting. As he moved, he kept a beam of ice on the serpent, freezing over its tail all the way to its neck. Now all the arrow needed to do was hit.

The serpent, in one final move, turned its head around and opened its mouth, swallowing the ice arrow. Damian gasped as it swallowed it. But then the serpent opened its mouth again, spewing vapor out. The arrow slowly froze the beast from the inside, letting ice choke it out. The beast roared, and that was it. It was frozen. Trina yanked her sword out and climbed down to the neck of the serpent. She swung the sword, and it slit the snake's throat. The serpent then disappeared with a puff of smoke.

Her job done, Trina exited out of Damian's mind.

Trina opened her eyes, looking straight into Damian's eyes. They were wide open, and Trina could tell he was wondering why he was on the ground, pinned down by glowing chains, with three of his teammates beside him. Standing up, Trina released the chains, helping Damian up. "What just happened?" Damian asked. "All I remember is fighting a giant black snake with a bow and arrow. And you guys were there."

"That was all inside your head," Trina explained. "You were taken over by some black-creature thingy. You attacked us, and we fought you. Then I pinned you down and entered your head with the help of the girls. We then fought off the creature, and you were freed."

Ashleigh and Jessica glanced at each other, chorusing, "It was mostly Trina." Then all of a sudden, a blue streak flashed and landed beside the four. Heat emanated from the figure, warming the four kids up. But when they looked closer, they realized that the figure was—Max! With flaming blue hair, orange eyes, and a silver spandex one-piece with orange stripes down the sides? *And* silver high-tops? This was too good to be true. Ah, the wonders of spandex. Boy, Trina would have to ask him about *this* major makeover. Max ran a hand through his hair, and his appearance changed back to normal (sadly). No more spandex, no flaming hair, no orange eyes, just Max with his regular blond hair.

"Aww, I was getting used to the spandex," Trina whined.

Max flushed pink. "W-well, the spandex wasn't my choice! And I'm not even sure it's spandex!"

"Sure," Trina smirked.

Max face-palmed and turned toward Ashleigh, who was gazing at him, mouth open. "Um, Ashleigh?" Max raised an eyebrow.

"Mm?" Ashleigh said distractedly. Then she regained her composure. "Huh, what?"

Everyone laughed, grinning widely. Then Trina's mind dipped into the dark side. "All right, all in favor of the flaming hair and silver spandex, raise your hand!" Trina smirked evilly.

The kids all raised their hands—except for Max, of course—and Max brought out a hair-dye spray bottle. It was slightly smaller than his hand, but he sprayed his hair with it, and with the now flaming hair came the silver spandex! Trina decided she needed to get spandex for her own costume because it hugs every darn curve of your body! "Woo! Spandex is back, baby!" she exclaimed cheerfully.

Max rolled his eyes.

Then Damian said, "I hate to be the voice of death, but don't we need to go after the *Warsnake*?"

"Oh, thank the heavens that Connor went after it!" Trina sighed.

"Well, we still need to go after them. Connor might be losing speed," Ashleigh pointed out.

"Good point," Jessica agreed.

"There's no time to fly, so I'll teleport us all to the *Warsnake*." Trina prepared a portal. The group walked into it and appeared inside the *Warsnake* moments later. A few aliens walked past the kids but apparently didn't see them because they continued their rounds. These aliens were different from the other ones the kids had seen. They had black feathery wings, retractable claws on their fingertips, and black sclerae that were completely devoid of life. The kids snuck past the guards and met up with Connor, who was busy trying to pick the lock of one of the captives' cells.

"Boo," Damian whispered into Connor's ear. He jumped and almost dropped the key he had made out of rock. He then glanced at Max behind them and raised an eyebrow.

"Later," Max dismissed him.

Connor resumed his previous attempts at unlocking the cell.

"Quickly," Damian warned. "There're guards coming for their rounds here."

Connor nodded and finally opened the cell door.

The alien captive seemed to be about five years older than Damian. It was a he, and he had dark-blue eyes and raven black hair that was cut into a comb-over. He raised his head at Connor and smiled, and it looked as if he hadn't smiled in months. Damian out-stretched his hand to him and pulled him up to his feet. Max asked, "Which planet are you fro—"

"Glacies-9." Damian interrupted.

"Okay," Max said. "What's your name?"

Before the boy could answer, thirteen armed sentries stormed the chamber, plasma rays blazing. The sentries aimed their rays at the now free captive, unleashing beams of plasma directed straight at him.

"You're not dying today!" Max exclaimed as he jumped in the way. The plasma beams were hot, but he could handle them. He collected all of the heat energy from the plasma, then expelled it in a fire wave. The sentries fell back, apparently regrouping, because moments later, the chamber was flooded with sentries! There were sentries to Max's right, guards to his left, and another group of sentries behind him. Ugh. Max hoped he never had to face them again.

The sentries aimed their plasma rays at Max, firing not a moment later. Max jumped into the air, doing a flip. But the Glacian alien stood his ground. With only a slight shift in his posture, ice raised out of the ground and curved around him, blocking the plasma blasts.

"Look out below!" Max yelled, raising a colossal fireball.

The Glacian alien twisted the ice around himself, forming a thick dome. Max threw the fireball down, and it slammed into the sentries, the ground, and the ice dome, destroying all of them. *Wow,* the Glacian thought, *he's powerful.* Max dropped down beside him, grinning. A few more sentries advanced toward the two, but the Glacian quickly trapped them in ice.

Now that the kids had defeated the sentries, they had one pressing matter to attend to.

"What's your name?" Max asked the Glacian.

"I don't remember. I've been trapped here for the most part of my life," the boy responded.

Max put a finger to his chin. "What if we call you Gavin?" Max asked.

"Gavin," the Glacian pondered. "Sure!"

Grinning, the team moved forward, hoping to destroy the *Warsnake.* They dashed through the hallways toward the control room, where the digital control pad was. They hoped beyond hope that once they made it to the control room, they could mess with the controls, destroy them, and send the *Warsnake* on a crash course to…somewhere. They opened a door and walked into the control room to look for the master control. After a couple seconds, Connor spotted the controls, calling the rest of the team to them. Without so much as a syllable, Damian and Gavin teamed up to create layers of frost on the controls, rendering them useless.

The master controls were frozen, and the kids were now going for the minor controls. Damian and Gavin stepped forward to freeze the controls, but Max interfered and scorched the control pad. Damian and Gavin froze the remains, and they tried to walk out, but a certain someone had something different in mind. The leader of the *Warsnake* sentries and guards had walked into the room! He was wearing black sweatpants.

"I see that you have busied yourselves with destroying my controls to this cargo ship," the commander spoke calmly.

"Uh, we, uh…," Ashleigh stuttered.

"Don't tell me what I already know," the commander commanded. Ashleigh shut her mouth.

Max glanced at Gavin, gesturing to the door. "Get out of here. Hide, escape, whatever! Just go. It's not safe here."

Without warning, the commander lunged at Ashleigh, right as Gavin ran through the door.

Ashleigh jumped and pirouetted in the air to dodge the attack. The commander unsheathed a black broadsword and threw it at Ashleigh's head. Trina slowed down time as she jumped to intercept the sword. She grabbed the hilt of the sword and pulled it down by her waist. She reset time, and the commander dropped to the ground as Ashleigh landed a roundhouse kick to his stomach.

"Aww, so easily defeated?" Ashleigh mocked.

The commander wordlessly moved behind her and placed a device on her back. Ashleigh started to expel electricity everywhere. You know what she looked like? A star on the verge of a supernova. Plus, her face? It was totally priceless! Ahem, not that having a teammate getting hurt is funny, ahem.

Commander Sweatpants removed the device from Ashleigh and threw it randomly into the air. Somehow the device managed to fly over to Damian. *Why me!* Damian cried as the device landed on his arm. The air temperature dropped by seventy degrees as part of Damian's life energy was stolen. The device unlatched itself from Damian's arm. Now it went over to Max. Oh, but Max wasn't having any of this! Max engulfed the wretched device in blue flames, and the device simply sucked up all the fire. It left Max alone and moved on to Jessica. Jessica formed a protective water bubble around herself, but the device sucked the water and left her. *Dun-dun-dunnn.*

It flew over to Trina, but she fed it her energy sword. Finally, it came to Connor. He created a ball of energy, and the device consumed it. But apparently, he was its dessert because it crawled onto his leg and feasted on his life energy. He felt absolutely drained.

The device flew back into Sweatpant-man's hand. He threw it on the ground, and it smashed into a zillion pieces. The energy was released like a bomb! It threw all the kids back into the walls, which was painful. Why was everything in life so painful? Connor slowly opened the door and crawled out. The others followed closely. Trina was directly behind Connor, followed by Max, Ashleigh, Damian, and Jessica.

Then Connor had a fantastic idea! "Trina, why don't you teleport us where we need to go?" Connor asked.

"Don't you think that I've also been weakened by that crazy device?" she responded irritably, simply looking for an excuse.

"All right, all right! I wasn't trying to annoy you," Connor relented. Jessica, Max, Damian, and Ashleigh charged into Trina as Connor grabbed her wrist. Trina faltered for a second but accidentally teleported them to someplace inside the planet.

Getting to his feet, Connor spotted the *Warsnake* coming up ahead! He raised a rock wall at the same time as Damian placed two giant ice blocks in front of him.

The *Warsnake* was getting closer! Trina slowed down time *around* the *Warsnake* so that they would have a little bit more of it to stop. The group scattered behind the rock wall to hide until the *Warsnake* made impact. Okay, now the *Warsnake* had hit the ice blocks. And...impact! Max and Connor flew out from behind the wall and started attacking the *Warsnake*! Max coated its outer metal with flames, and Ashleigh focused beams of electricity on the places where Max had hit. Max punched the left side of the *Warsnake* and left an orange glowing fist mark. It glowed brighter and brighter and brighter until it exploded! *Boom-boom!*

But this was not your regular alien cargo ship. This snake thingy was built for war! You could call it anything but a cargo ship. What "cargo ship" can shoot lava out of its metal scales/armor? What "cargo ship" doesn't get a scratch even when its side explodes? What "cargo ship"—you get the idea. The *Warsnake* sprayed lava everywhere, singeing clothes and whatnot!

"Oh no!" Damian, Trina, Jessica, and Ashleigh exclaimed in unison. Max and Connor just stared at them. Connor had a light-green shirt and tight silver pants to go with it, both made with Naturaean fabric. But somehow the shirt and pant had been sown together with the same light-green fabric as the shirt, creating a one-piece. On the middle of his shirt, Connor wore a silver emblem. It was a circle about two inches in diameter, with three leaves: one leaf in the middle of the circle, one going diagonally to the right, and one going diagonally to the left. This emblem was the symbol of Naturae-37. Also, Connor wore a dark-green cape.

My clothing is indestructible, so I have nothing to worry about, Connor thought.

But then Trina sighed, interrupting Connor's thoughts. "I'll stitch."

The *Warsnake* flew away quickly. You've got to give it credit for sensing an opening. Trina created a needle and yellow thread and started stitching Ashleigh's singed jeggings. When she was done, Ashleigh didn't have her regular blue jeggings and gray T-shirt anymore. Trina had made bright-yellow leggings with black stripes on the sides and a yellow short-sleeved dress that had a black line spiraling from Ashleigh's neck around her back and to her waist. The cape was black. Trina flicked her wrist, and small shiny golden jewels lined up on the shoulder parts of Ashleigh's shirt. With another wave of her hand, Ashleigh's normally raven-black hair got a gold streak down the middle and was pulled back into a high ponytail! How cool is that? The last thing Trina did was change Ashleigh's blue sneakers into purple wedge boots!

"Wow. You are good. Thanks!" Ashleigh said happily.

Now it was Jessica's turn for a major makeover. Trina changed the thread color to dark blue and started stitching Jessica's clothing. When she was done, Jessica wasn't wearing skinny jeans and a T-shirt. She wore a shimmering royal-blue cape dress with jewels on the sides. She also wore azure-blue leggings with two aqua-blue stripes parting in the middle. Her hairstyle changed into a french braid down her shoulder, and there was blue hair dye spiraling down it. She looked amazing!

"The best part is, they're indestructible," Trina said proudly.

"Wow!" Jessica stared in awe. Trina snapped her fingers, and Jessica's red tennis shoes turned into black knee-high wedge boots. Trina made the boots somewhat stretchy and tight so that they didn't fan out at the top. Jessica was now speechless. Finally she regained her speech. "Wow," she said, "this one's even better than Ashleigh's."

"Oh no, you didn't!" A loud *smack!* could be heard halfway across the planet.

Damian was next. Trina used a celeste-blue thread this time. She stitched and stitched and stitched some more, and finally she was done. Damian now wore a celeste-blue spandex one-piece with two gray stripes that started from his shoulders and formed a *V* near the middle of his rib cage. He had a blue gemstone where his neckline was, and he also wore knee-high black sneakers. His cape billowed behind him.

"Darn, Ashleigh has a powerful arm," Max muttered to Damian.

"Tell me about it," Damian replied.

Jessica rubbed her right cheek where Ashleigh had slapped her. "Jeez, I wasn't trying to be mean or anything!"

"Next time, try saying it nicely," Ashleigh snapped.

Trina motioned for Max to step up, and when he did, she added an orange cape to his one-piece spandex. Trina then helped herself, remaking her cape. She recreated her shirt, giving it a darker shade of pink and making it a long-sleeve. Her leggings turned pink, glitter shining in random spots. Then shiny aqua-green gems appeared, creating trails down her arms and legs. A sheath appeared at her waist, and her energy sword slid in.

"All right. Now that we know what Trina's future job will be, can we get going? We have a couple thousand planets to save," Ashleigh said impatiently, watching as the needle and colorful thread disappeared.

"Agreed. Let's get going," Trina replied coolly. And they took off after the *Warsnake*.

CHAPTER 11

The Bad Guys Go Boom-Boom!

Trina opened a portal, gesturing for the others to get in. They all stepped in, appearing on the land above. Ah, land at last. "There!" Connor said, pointing into the sky.

They all glanced upward, spotting the *Warsnake* just disappearing over the horizon. Trina grinned. "Time for round two." Trina then launched herself into the sky, going after the *Warsnake*.

Connor molded the obsidian under his feet, crafting a surfboard. He then took off after Trina. Everyone else followed him, ready to destroy the 'Snake once and for all.

Trina was the first to land on the *Warsnake*. She lowered herself to one of the lava flaps, unsheathing her sword. She placed it in between a flap, enlarging it to create a large enough space for the kids to get in. Then the rest of the team dropped beside her.

"I see you've been helping," Connor said.

Trina winked, grabbing her sword and climbing into the space.

They slipped inside, taking in their surroundings as Trina sheathed her sword. But before anyone could do anything, an alarm sounded. "The flaps have been breached! The flaps have been breached! Burn the infiltrators!"

Only moments after the alarm was issued, the small space started to flood with lava.

"Back up!" Trina yelled. She placed her hands on the ground, and an energy wall raised out of the ground and blocked the flow in front of them. But then lava started to fill the space behind them. Connor grabbed his surfboard and stuck it into the ground, expanding it. The obsidian stretched out in seconds, blocking the lava flow.

"We need to get out of here," Max said, eyeing the lava. "We don't know what could happen next. But first, I'll destroy this chamber."

As Trina blinked, Max jumped onto the top part of the chamber, landing several glowing punches to it. Then he hit the ground, leaving glowing marks as he ran. He got to both ends of the chamber, leaving, orange fist marks. Done with the first part of his plan, Max nodded at Trina. Trina raised her arms, and a portal appeared in front of them. The kids quickly hustled into the glowing mass, reappearing in the now destroyed control room.

"Count down from three," Max said.

Shrugging, the kids counted. "Three." Max cracked his knuckles. "Two."

What is Max doing? Connor wondered.

"One."

Max clenched his fists, and a split second later, a loud *BOOM!* shook the *Warsnake*.

"Max," Trina started, "did you just take out one of the lava flaps with a bunch of perfectly timed explosions?"

Max stroked his chin. "When you put it that way, it makes it sound like I'm some genius. But yes."

Trina glanced from Max to the others' unimpressed expressions. Minus Connor anyway. "How come you guys aren't even slightly impressed?" she asked.

"Because," Jessica answered, "that is really not his most powerful ability. What would have made it cooler was if he'd taken it out with *one* punch."

Ashleigh and Damian nodded in agreement.

Then before anyone could say or do anything, the door burst open, and a sentry rushed in, saying, "Run! He's coming for you. You need to get out!" Then the sentry turned around and gasped, disappearing.

The kids turned around just as a metal fist shot toward them. Thinking on her feet, Ashleigh caught the fist with her right hand, grabbing the arm with her left. She twisted her hands over her head, sending the figure crashing into control panels behind her. The kids moved backward as the figure lifted itself off the controls.

"You are fools to return," a deep slightly electronic voice said.

Ashleigh recognized the voice. She'd heard it somewhere—then it dawned on her. "Sweatpants!" she cried, and the others understood.

"That guy again?" Damian asked. Ashleigh nodded.

"If I were to assume, I'd say this guy is dangerous, and we need to leave," Max said.

"And if I were to assume, I'd say that the time it takes for me to open a portal would be enough for him to massacre us," Trina said.

"Is that what we're calling it now? A massacre?" Ashleigh added.

"I'll buy you time," Max said. "Go!"

Trina nodded, leading everyone except Max out of the room or so she thought.

"Ashleigh, you need to go too," Max said, not removing his eyes from his opponent.

"Oh?" Ashleigh sounded. "Last I remember, we make a pretty good team."

Max rolled his eyes. "Fine."

"That's the spirit!" Ashleigh said cheerily. She stood behind Max, watching the commander. Moving one hand behind himself, Max counted down on his fingers from five.

A pair of daggers appeared in Ashleigh's hands on the count of four, two lightning clones with daggers of their own appearing on two. Max hit one, and the kids sprung at the commander.

Ashleigh's clones jumped into the air above the commander, slicing at him with their daggers. The commander caught the two, launching them at Max and Ashleigh. The pair sidestepped the projectiles, rushing forward. Ashleigh threw one of her daggers, creating another one almost instantly. The dagger flew through the air at what seemed like a hundred miles per hour, leaving a yellow trail of electricity in its wake. It closed in fast—fifteen feet, fourteen feet, thirteen feet, twelve feet, eleven feet, ten feet, nine feet, eight feet, seven feet, six feet, five feet, four feet, three feet, two feet, one foot. But right before the dagger could hit the commander's armor, he raised a black circular shield.

The dagger slammed into the shield, making a loud CLANG! sound. Ashleigh narrowed her eyes in frustration, channeling her energy into her hands. As she dropped her daggers and clenched her fists, yellow glowing electricity flowed around them, strengthening them. Ashleigh jumped forward and slammed her right fist into the shield, creating an electric shock wave from the impact. But although her attack didn't hit, it distracted the commander long enough for Max to jump up from behind Ashleigh and place his hands on the commander's head.

Max then twisted around the commander, wrapping his legs around the commander's neck. He then began striking everywhere on the commander's head, slightly denting the metal armor. The commander dropped his shield and yanked at Max's legs, trying to pull him off. Ashleigh took the opportunity and moved several meters backward, realizing that the commander's stomach area was exposed. Ashleigh lifted off the ground, creating a small version of her avatar around herself. She then shot forward, slicing through the air.

To the commander, everything seemed to be moving in slow motion. Ashleigh pulled her fist back, increasing her speed. At the same time, Max slid off the commander's head, landing glowing blows anywhere he could hit. As Max's feet hit the ground, fiery tendrils shot out of the ground and wrapped around the commander's legs, locking him in place. More tendrils snaked around the commander's arms, ensuring that he wouldn't block the attack. Ashleigh closed the gap between herself and the commander, launching her fist forward.

The impact of the punch was insane. The commander's body wanted to move backward from the force of the punch, but the tendrils holding him wouldn't let him move an inch. All he could do was cry out in pain as the armor protecting his abdomen shattered. From the amount of pain he was feeling, he could have safely assumed that Ashleigh had ruptured all the organs near his stomach.

But the commander was not scared now. Rage overtook him, numbing the pain and sharpening his senses. Whatever the pair had done to him, he would do it back tenfold. Max glanced at Ashleigh, and the message was clear as glass: *We need to leave.* Max took off running out of the room, Ashleigh in tow. He frantically glanced down the hallway as he heard the commander roar in anger behind him.

"There!" Ashleigh yelled, pointing to a pink swirling portal to their left.

The two ran like their lives depended on it—they really did—making a mad dash toward the portal. The commander didn't waste time, going after them just as quickly. "We can't have him following us," Ashleigh said. "We need to do something."

"Are you nuts!" Max exclaimed. "We stop running now, we die. Boom. End of story."

"But if we don't stop him, he'll get into the portal with us, and he could go on a rampage through New York," Ashleigh reasoned.

"And if we die, he'll still make it in!" Max yelled exasperatedly. The portal was only a few meters away. If they were to make a decision, they had to make it now.

"Fine, I'll stop him, and you go," Ashleigh said, about to turn around.

"Not on my watch," Max said, grabbing her arm as he jumped into the portal. Ashleigh was the only one that saw that the commander made it in with them.

"Where are they?" Damian wondered aloud as he stared into the other end of the portal Trina had made. "They said they were going to buy us some time, that's all!"

Then two figures shot out of the portal. "Max, Ashleigh!" the team chorused joyfully.

But Ashleigh wasn't having it. "There's no time to celebrate! The commander made it in with us." Right after the words left her mouth, the commander walked out of the portal, cackling.

"Fools." The commander outstretched his left hand, and a ball of fire grew. He threw the fireball at Ashleigh, but Max stepped in the way, absorbing the flames.

Max held a serious look on his face, the one that said, *Try to hurt my friends again, and you will die.* But when he saw the orange glowing marks on the commander's armor, he couldn't help but smile.

"You called us fools, yet you couldn't even see the orange glowing fist marks all over you," Max said. "And even if you did, you should have known that it wasn't just a decoration." Max clenched his fist, and the marks glowed brighter, exploding all over the commander.

The commander flew forward, the force from the explosions shoving him to the ground. His armor was cracked in several places and was, in a couple spots, shattered. Max didn't waste a second, engulfing the commander in flames. But Max was surprised to watch the commander rise to his feet, pushing the fire away. Before Max could react, the commander shot forward, grabbing Max's neck. Max's eyes widened as he tugged at the commander's hands, desperately trying to regain his ability to breathe.

Trina jumped forward, unsheathing her sword. She swung at the commander, but he used his free hand to block it. The commander then slammed Max into the ground, dragging him as he broke into a sprint. Jessica quickly wrapped several water chains around the commander, holding him back. Damian froze the chains, locking the commander. Connor disappeared into the ground, reappearing in between Max and the commander. Before anyone blinked, Connor landed a swift uppercut to the commander's chin, loosening his grip on Max.

Meanwhile, Max's vision was swimming. *It's really funny*, Max thought to himself, *that a dozen punches won't kill me. A dozen stabs probably won't kill me either. A nuke wouldn't kill me. But I'd die from loss of air! Air!* Max's vision faded, but he fought to keep his eyes open. He felt his back hit the ground, felt the pain of the sharp rocks and stones on his back. But what could he do? *Maybe I can finally have peace*, he thought, shutting his eyes. Then he blacked out as the commander let go of him.

At that sight, the others went berserk. Ashleigh launched herself at the commander, tackling him. She slammed her fists into his exposed abdomen, making him cry out with every hit. "You"—punch—"just"—punch—"killed"—punch—"Max!" *Hulk smash!*

Trina placed her hands on the ground, and pink chains wrapped themselves around the commander. "You disgust me," she spat, punching the commander in the gut. Connor glared at the commander with venom in his eyes, and I'll tell you this: if looks could kill, the commander would be slowly dying, writhing in agony as venomous snakes bit him.

Jessica placed her hands on a spot on the commander's helmet that had cracked open. "Max died from loss of air," she said. "So that's how you'll go too." She poured water into the helmet, filling it up. Then Trina sealed the helmet with energy, letting him drown. The commander's eyes widened, and he shook his head, trying to escape. But it was futile. He couldn't move his arms, couldn't move his legs, nothing. And there was no one to help him.

After about thirty seconds, the commander inhaled water for the first time, exhaling water for the last. Water slowly filled his lungs, and he coughed, moving his mouth for the last time in his life.

At the same time, Trina moved over to Max, placing her hands to his chest. Though she had only seen people do it and never had done it herself, she began CPR. She created a plastic bag and breathed into it, pinching Max's nose and putting the opening of the plastic bag to Max's mouth. For a second, nothing happened. So Trina repeated the process. Then after a couple tries, Max coughed, eyes fluttering.

His head was throbbing, and his back was sore. At first everything around him glowed, and the pain was gone. *I'm in heaven!* he thought. Then his vision focused, and the pain returned. He could now make out his friends' figures and Trina's face above him. Then memories flooded his mind—how he'd been fighting the commander, but he'd choked him, and then he blacked out. Then he remembered something else. There was one mark he'd left on the commander that he hadn't blown up.

Max clenched his fist, and the mark exploded, sending the commander's body flying into the air. Jessica cleared her throat as she saw the explosion. "Today is an important day," she began, "because the bad guys go boom-boom. Poof! Just like that." The kids all laughed.

But then Jessica saw Max's eyes widen. "Look out!" Max said, pointing at a fiery object hurtling toward them. Trina scrambled to her feet, trying to lift Max up.

"Run, guys!" were Trina's last words as she blacked out.

CHAPTER 12

How Lil Bro Saved Our Butts

Ugh. My head is throbbing. *What the…wait, where on earth are we?* was what Trina was thinking, but through an apparent telepathic link, all the kids could communicate silently.

Umm, more importantly, why are you in my head? was Damian's reply.

Did you really just ask me why I'm in your head? she asked.

What do you think? thought Damian.

Because, Damian, I'm Trina. If that doesn't answer your question, then nothing will.

Guys, where are we? thought Max.

Yeah, where are we? thought Ashleigh.

What she said, thought Connor. *I agree with the rest of you.*

I don't know! I'm as confused as you are. Oh, and by the way, why are you using my head as a walkie-talkie? Trina asked.

No idea, Jessica thought blankly.

Damian opened his eyes and tried to stand up. His surroundings were mostly black, but there were five beams of light around him. As his vision adjusted to the lack of light, he found that in all of those five beams of light, there were five people—no, kids who were in cages. He looked down at his feet and found that he was *also* in a cage. You cannot understand the frustration he felt when he saw that. All the cages were square, with CD-sized holes on the ground and on the sides. Damian groaned loudly and tried to punch his way through the metal bars. Nothing happened. He backed up as far as he could, which was only a couple feet, and rammed his shoulder into the bars. This time, the cage shrank, and he had to squat in order to fit inside it. "Urgh," he growled loudly.

Max squinted from a cage in front of him. "Damian," he whispered, "what did they do to you?"

Now Damian felt a wave of pain take over his body. His mouth felt dry. "D-do what?" He felt his arms and face—he was bleeding from a cut on his left arm and another on his cheek. He could feel a bruise on his forehead too. But when he looked closer, he noticed that all his cuts were slowly closing. The cuts were shrinking, replaced by regular skin. *That's never happened before*, Damian thought to himself. But before he could ponder the subject further, somebody asked, "Do you think they're conscious?" The person had a high-pitched female voice.

"Nah, they're sure to be collapsed on the ground," responded a low male voice.

"How much are you willing to bet?" the female asked.

"I'll bet you one hundred thousand ne'ans that they're unconscious," the male answered confidently.

"Promise?" the female asked.

"Deal," the male agreed. The pair walked inside the room and stared at the kids.

"Well, well, well," the female started, "they're conscious. Looks like you owe me one hundred thousand ne'ans, Rorinn."

"My fingers were crossed, Allaya!" Rorinn swore.

Allaya's face darkened, and wind began to swirl around her. Her long silver hair floated in the air. "You'd better give me what you owe me!" Allaya growled.

Rorinn wasn't fazed. "Allaya, we have a job to do."

Allaya raised her arms, and two giant wind arms curled around Rorinn. *She gets triggered so easily.* Rorinn sighed.

Meanwhile, the kids conversed in their heads. *They're distracted*, Damian thought.

We have an opening. Maybe we can escape while they're fighting over there, Trina strategized.

I have a plan, Jessica said. *You see that key hanging from Allaya's neck?* Everyone glanced at Allaya, watching as it swung from side to side. *If my assumption is correct, that key unlocks these cages. From here, I can tell that it's the same shape as the lock. We won't be able to use our powers 'cause they're being restrained. I can feel it. So I'll make a ruckus. Get Allaya to come down to my level, then stick my arm out and grab the key. Then I'll unlock my cage and free you guys.*

Sounds like a plan, they all agreed.

Allaya squeezed Rorinn with a wind arm. "Give. Me. My. Money."

Rorinn shook his head, turning pitch-black and slipping out of the restraint.

Allaya huffed. "This always happens! We make a bet, I win the bet, and you refuse to keep to your own end of it!"

Before Rorinn could respond, a voice called, "Hey! Bet breaker!"

Rorinn and Allaya turned around to see Jessica facing them. "Allaya, I feel for you. Boys just can't seem to follow the rules," Jessica said with disgust.

Allaya nodded. "I know, right? They never keep promises, and they're just so annoying!"

Jessica gestured to Max, Connor, and Damian. "You see those three? They're real idiots too. It's hard to believe that geniuses like us"—Jessica gestured to Ashleigh, Trina, and Allaya—"are stuck with them. But come here. I have a secret to tell you. This one trick always gets them to listen."

Intrigued, Allaya moved toward Jessica's cage. Unbeknownst to her, this was all part of Jessica's plan. Allaya leaned down as Jessica moved her hands and face to Allaya's ear. But then Jessica shot out her right hand and yanked the key from Allaya's neck. Before Allaya could react, Jessica punched her on the chin, knocking her out.

Jessica shoved the key into the lock, turning it to the left. Her cage swung open, and she dashed to Trina's cage. She twisted the key, and the cage opened with a *click!* sound. Rorinn dashed at Jessica, raising his fist. But before he could hit Jessica, Trina jumped in the way, kicking the man in the stomach. Rorinn was sent sprawling onto the ground several meters away. Trina noted this, realizing that even the strongest of humans wouldn't be able to hit *that* hard.

"It seems as if our elemental powers are the only things being restrained," Trina said.

Jessica nodded, unlocking Ashleigh's cage. She then moved on to Connor's, then Max's, then Damian's. Finally, the whole team was free.

Rorinn sent a punch flying at Trina's face, but she caught it with her left hand. With her right hand, she punched Rorinn in the gut, kneeing him in the groin. Roninn's eyes widened, and he fell to the ground. *She's fast!* he thought. *She didn't even give me time to switch to my shadow form.*

Then an idea formed in Trina's head. She grabbed Roninn by his wrists, picking Allaya up, and shoved them into separate cages. She then closed the cages and locked them in, leaving them there for someone to find. Eventually.

Then four shadows moved toward the door, revealing themselves as they walked in: sentries. "Jeez!" the middle one said. "What happen—" He stopped.

"Trina?" the sentry asked. "Is that you?"

Trina took a step back, confused. "How do you know my name? And why do you sound like my brother?"

Brother? the rest of the team thought. *She has a brother?*

The sentry pulled off his helmet, revealing a boy with raven-black hair, about the same age as the kids. His skin was light brown, the same color as Trina's, and his eyes were light gray. Trina's eyes widened, and she let out a name on a single breath. "Ronan."

"Trina," Ronan said, walking forward. Then the two siblings hugged each other, chorusing, "I thought you were dead."

"Sorry to break up the family reunion," Damian said, "but that looks just like a speedster with wind powers named Noran!"

Trina raised an eyebrow, wondering what on earth her teammates could be talking about. Then Max said, "That's because the name *Noran* was an anagram. This *is* Noran."

"Speedster? Wind powers?" Trina asked.

Ronan scratched his head sheepishly. "Well, you see, I got powers, like you. Except I have wind and superspeed powers." Yells echoed through the halls. "And we need to leave. Like right now."

Damian rubbed his wrists. "How do we escape? They shut off our flight powers. I can feel it."

Ronan seemed to consider this. Ronan strapped his bow to his back, and a sly grin came to his mouth. "All right. How good are y'all at flying things?"

They all raced through the halls, narrowly missing a squad of soldiers that rushed into the room. Ronan's team of archers helped the kids escape. They entered a large chamber where ten black vehicles sat parked. They looked like motorcycles but slimmer. There was definitely more to them than met the eye. Ronan whispered a code, and they shuddered to life. The kids mounted them and put on the helmets that waited on the seats. Ronan clicked a button on his belt, and the emergency escape hatch swung open. He put a hand to his helmet, and static crackled in the kids' ears. Apparently, the helmets also had speakers.

"Swipe two fingers on the control pad," Ronan said over the helmet speakers. They swiped the screens, and the motorcycle lights flickered on. "The lights are projected from the bulbs inside that transparent metal," Ronan explained. "Now click the red button. The Starcycle should show a holographic map of space—including where we are and where Earth is."

They clicked the buttons eagerly, and the map popped up. The handlebar extended from the front. They put their feet into the footrests and revved the engines. Shouts of people and pounding feet rang through the chamber. The soldiers were getting close.

"Click the autopilot button!" Ronan yelled anxiously.

Once they had clicked autopilot, they zoomed off into space. Over a hundred soldiers bust through the door just as the kids made their escape. They tapped their helmets, and metal glider wings shot out from jetpacks on their backs. They gave chase, and the kids had to split up.

"Don't stray far!" Damian said through the speaker. "Now let's see what this baby can do," he whispered to himself. He swiped through the screen and looked for a weaponry listing. Thankfully, he found it! Sadly, it beeped: *autopilot deactivated*. The screen read: "heat-seeking missiles, laser cannon, and EMP cannon."

"Perfect." Damian struck with the missiles first. Seven missiles flew at the closest soldiers to him. *Seven down, twenty to go*, he thought. Next, Damian fired the laser cannon. It took out around ten of them. Lastly, he used the EMP cannon. It sent out a wave of electromagnetic energy and disarmed the rest. He fell back into the group. "Did you miss me?" he asked smugly.

Ignoring him, Ronan scrolled through his map and said, "Earth is close up ahead. Prepare yourselves for reentry." They rocketed past Jupiter and blew past Mars, nearing Earth rapidly. Damian swiped quickly through the modes, searching for any shields. Luckily, there were many shields: some for lasers, others for projectiles, but more importantly, four of them were for reentry. "Go into the modes, find the shields, and click on the *X* symbol on the screen!" Damian yelled. They followed his instructions, and white shields appeared in front of the Starcycles.

The kids dove down into the Earth's atmosphere and started to accelerate. The shields were burning up rapidly, and Damian doubted they would last long enough to land.

"Guys, pull up!" Ronan screeched. The maps switched from outer space to Earth. Surprisingly, the map showed text in bold, and it read: WARNING, ALTITUDE DECREASING RAPIDLY! That was sort of depressing. The handlebars switched for a steering wheel that seriously looked just like a 2018 Tesla Roadster's.

"This is 2088, for crying out loud! Unacceptable!" Ashleigh quipped.

"Well, it's better than nothing," Damian murmured.

Damian tried pulling at the steering wheel, but nothing happened! The screen beeped. *Thirty seconds until impact*. Then it started counting down from thirty.

"Do something!" Ashleigh yelled over the speaker.

"What do you take me for? Poseidon?" Damian retorted, annoyed. *Twenty seconds until impact*. Damian looked at the ground and saw helpless civilians staring up in horror. They were probably thinking that the kids would hit them. Damian swiped the screen and searched for any auto-alignment. *Ten seconds.*

Damian finally found it. Ronan slowed the group down with his wind abilities, but he could only do so much. Damian activated the auto-alignment, and the Starcycle gradually pulled itself out from its nosedive. The others followed suit, and soon they had landed.

"We need to park these things somewhere," Damian pointed out.

"Way ahead of you." Connor raised a tall earthen building, and wheels sprouted on the Starcycles where they would have been on a real motorcycle. They drove into the building and disappeared behind its rock walls, parking. The kids then removed their helmets and placed them back on the seats, sighing in relief.

Then Jessica had an idea. "You know, this place could be—"

"Our base!" Max interrupted.

"Yes," Jessica hissed, giving Max a glare that screamed certain death.

"Anyway, we could have this as a central headquarters. Oh, and we could also use our current *awesome* technology to find more heroes. I doubt we're the only ones."

"Yeah! Adding metal would work! Because all of us have metal powers!" Ronan said sarcastically.

Deciding to not let the conversation escalate, Connor created a door in front of the Starcycles. "Let's go," he said.

All seven kids and the three archers who'd followed them managed to fit through the narrow doorway. When they were all inside the space, Connor flicked his hand upward, and the ground lifted them up into...somewhere. It was kind of like an elevator, except it was rockier.

When the "elevator" finally stopped, a door appeared beside Connor and the group walked through. They stepped into a spacious place that looked like it could fit hundreds of people. It was big.

"So, Connor, you're telling me that you created this building two minutes ago?" Trina spoke.

"Yep!" Connor replied happily.

"Amazing," Trina muttered.

Connor stared at the wall, and a seven-foot-long earthen control pad rose out of the ground, though there were no electronics. There were depressions where electronics were supposed to be, and Connor seemed to notice Jessica's curiosity. "Oh, yeah. We need someone to create those 'electronics' you speak of."

"Can we move this building out of the *middle* of Manhattan?" Ashleigh asked, though it was more an order, if anything.

Connor concentrated on the ground, and the building shuddered.

"Wha—" Jessica was cut off by Damian crashing into her.

He stood up awkwardly. "S-sorry," he stuttered.

The entire building shook, and the kids were overcome by the sensation that they were on an airplane of some kind. It felt like it was taking off, but there were no seat belts. In desperation for something to hold on to, Jessica tried to grab Ronan's arm, but a sudden lurch flung the kids all over the place.

With her rotten luck, Jessica slammed into Trina, ending up in a pretzel with her and Ronan, and Ashleigh landed on top of one of Ronan's archers. Jessica rubbed her head. Damian helped her to her feet, and the shaking stopped.

"Thanks," Jessica mumbled.

But before anyone could do anything, Jessica got a weird watery feeling in her arms. "Where'd you set us down?" Jessica asked Connor.

Connor looked out of a crystal window. "I set it off the coast of Manhattan, in the Atlantic Ocean. Why?"

"Doesn't rock erode in water? However slowly?" Jessica remarked, worried.

"Oh, no worries. The bottom is made of crystal that won't erode," Connor said reassuringly.

Trina opened a medium-sized portal. "Ugh, finally!" she exclaimed, exasperated. "I've opened a portal, but it's very unstable."

Just as the kids tried to walk inside it, the portal collapsed and knocked all of them back with a wave of energy.

"*That* was helpful," Ashleigh muttered.

Trina crossed her arms. "Well, in my defense, I never said you could walk into it."

"Let's get out of here," Max declared, starting toward the sliding door of the elevator.

"No, we archers stay. We set up equipment here for you," one of Ronan's crew members said.

"But where would you get equi—oh, no. I won't allow you guys to go back *there*! They could *kill* you," Max said.

"No. Archers have skills. We go retrieve metal," the member said defiantly.

Max finally agreed. "All right, but be safe."

The archers nodded and walked into the elevator. Connor concentrated on the door, and the elevator launched itself down the building. They heard Starcycles revving and then driving out.

"I picture a story entitled 'How Lil Bro Saved Our Butts,'" Trina said, her thoughts coming into reality as images in the air. "Where it's about Ronan helping us escape from an evil lair of doom!"

Ashleigh pointed to Trina, then twirled her finger around in a circle. The others nodded in agreement.

"Well, we might as well plan for how we'll get our full powers back. And what better place to do it than here?" she pointed out.

"All right," the others agreed.

CHAPTER 13

A Completely Unnecessary Spider-Man Onesie

"We should take a break from those big heroics for now. Just rest up, everyone. We have a long way ahead of us," Damian said.

"But on top of resting, we also need to train. To get better with our powers," Trina said. "The way we are now, we don't stand a chance against the Ne'faro!"

"Ne'faro?" Damian asked. "What's the Ne'faro?"

"You know those blue-skinned aliens we keep encountering? That's them. They are the Ne'faro, a race of aliens that will stop at nothing to control everything," Trina explained.

"Not all of them are power-hungry and evil," Connor said. "I had a Ne'faro friend once. Good person, but I don't know what happened to him."

"But anyway," Trina continued, "we need to get stronger, faster, smarter. Even the odds. But first, we go to sleep!"

Connor raised his hand, and a sliding door appeared on the wall behind Damian. They walked through the door, and Trina made seven beds appear. She snapped her fingers, and the kids all got new changes of clothes, including her. Damian got his favorite elastic Superman shirt and stretchy jogger pants, and from what he could feel, he also got a clean change of underwear. Max rubbed his hand through his flaming hair, and his spandex suit disappeared with his flaming hair. Max had on a green T-shirt with orange stripes going diagonally and neon-yellow athletic pants. Ronan wore a red-and-blue Spider-man onesie, which was completely unnecessary. Connor wore a camouflage T-shirt and pants. The girls all wore onesies, each with their respective colors. Jessica was dark blue, Ashleigh was yellow, and Trina was pink. Trina's curly black hair was tied back into a ponytail. The kids laid down on their beds, and Connor made the ceiling turn into sand.

"Turn it to glass!" Connor told Max.

Max sent a steady stream of blue fire at the sand, turning it to molten sand. "Damian, Ronan, cool it down," Max said.

Damian and Ronan both sent waves of cold air at the molten sand, cooling it into glass. Now the kids had a way to see the night sky as they drifted off to sleep. A couple hours later, while the others were zonked out, Jessica and Damian stared up at the night sky, which was sprinkled with stars.

Right as Damian was about to fall asleep, a noise jolted him wide awake. Apparently, Jessica heard the noise because she asked, "What was that?"

"I don't know. But let's check it out," Damian said.

They silently sprang out of their beds and slid the door open.

Something rumbled again. Jessica grabbed Damian's hand. "Slowly," she cautioned. In her right hand, Damian saw water gather. His ice dagger materialized in his left.

"The elevator won't work if Connor isn't here. There's a door to your left," Damian whispered.

They opened the door and ran down the flight of stairs. Then as they got to the bottom stair, Damian was blinded by a powerful light! He threw his dagger blindly but heard something whistle through the air. The clinking of ice against metal was piercing. When the light dimmed, he saw the three archers, each wounded, but with the metal that they promised.

Jessica ran forward. "What happened to you?"

"They attacked us. Only three of us. Twelve of them. Was not fair fight," the lead archer said.

Using her left hand, Jessica applied water to their wounds. Damian could see them closing, slowly but surely. Jessica and Damian helped the archers carry the loads of metal to the control room.

When they had finished, there were seventeen piles of metal pieces. Each pile was at least as tall as Damian, who was four feet eight. The archers pulled out blowtorches and got to work. They mounted a three-foot stand in the middle indentation for the screen. They welded together a screen lining that was seventy-two inches long and thirty-six inches tall. The archers placed a screen inside the lining and connected a cable to the back of the screen. Since Trina had made the control pad metal, they made a hole for the cables and stuffed them inside.

"We also placed satellites above each"—the archer paused—"what do you call them? Oh! Yes! Continent," the archer said happily.

"That's amazing!" Jessica rejoiced. Soon the screen was showing the flying cars of Manhattan. "But now we have to get to bed. You guys comin'?" She yawned.

"No. We install more equipment," the archers chorused. With that, they got to work on what looked like an interface for the control pad.

Jessica opened the door. Trina and Ashleigh sat up in their beds. Eyebrows raised, they pulled up their blankets.

"We heard the archers come back and went to check it out," Damian whispered.

The girls exchanged looks and nodded back to sleep. Jessica and Damian slipped into their separate beds and snuggled up under the blankets.

Damian slept like a baby. He didn't dream or anything. Just a nice, peaceful sleep was what he needed.

Several hours later, Damian woke up. The rest of the team was up, and the sky was sunny. "What time is it?" Damian asked, rubbing his eyes.

Ashleigh pulled up the time on her smartwatch. "Nine forty-six."

"Okay," Damian muttered. He rolled out of bed and slipped into a pair of blue sneakers. He opened the door, sleep out of his system. "Guys, let's check everything out downstairs. I want to use the stairs anyway."

They raced down the flights of stairs and ended up in the main room. Everything looked amazing! They had a working screen projecting satellite images and zooming in on suspicious things.

"Woah"—Ashleigh gasped—"this is amazing!"

The archers huddled around a round table they set up. They yawned. "Thank you for help, you two." An archer pointed at Jessica and Damian.

"You're welcome," Jessica replied.

They shuffled up the stairs to their room, leaving the seven kids alone. Connor pinched one of the holographic controls, and the view of Manhattan sharpened. It zoomed in on one of the roads. There were people flying their cars and riding hovercycles on the street while civilians moved about on the sidewalks.

Then they saw one man. He was armed with a laser rifle and wore clearly high-tech armor. He opened the door of a bank, looked left and right, and walked in.

"He's going to rob Marlon Bank!" Damian gasped.

"We've gotta stop him," Jessica said.

Trina clapped, and the kids' regular clothes came on. Damian's blue spandex one-piece returned, along with his cape and black sneakers. Max sprayed his hair with the "magic" spray bottle, and his flaming blue hair returned. He donned his spandex one-piece and cape too. Ronan wore a gray spandex one-piece with large Xs on his thighs. He had a cape and gray knee-high sneakers. The girls' cape dresses returned, except this time, the dresses didn't stop at their shoulders and went halfway up their necks.

"Let's go," Damian said, racing down the stairs to the garage.

The team mounted the Starcycles, and the 2018 Tesla Roadster steering wheels appeared. They slipped on their helmets, and Connor lifted the garage entrance door as they flew out. The archers had somehow managed to connect the Starcycles to the satellite too, so they had clear views of the Marlon Bank. The wheels popped out, and they rounded Marvin Street, zooming past cars that were in driving mode. The GPS beeped: *Marlon Bank in one mile.* The team neared the bank. They would reach it in about a thousand yards.

After about thirty seconds of weaving through traffic, they drove into the parking lot of the bank and removed their helmets. They ran in through the back door and spotted the robber. He had one of the attendants on the ground at laserpoint, the weapon aimed at her head. "Give me all your money!" he roared.

Before the attendant could speak, Jessica extended her whip and pulled the laser rifle out of his hand. "Looking for somethin'?"

The robber turned as Jessica handed the rifle to Ashleigh. Ashleigh broke the rifle in two, dropping the pieces to the ground. The robber then realized that he was only facing a bunch of kids. "Stay out of my way, and you won't get hurt, little girl," he said, pointing at Ashleigh.

It took a second for Ashleigh to process the words the robber had just uttered. *Wait for it,* Max thought. *Wait for it.* Then it hit Ashleigh. "Little girl!" she screamed. *Got 'em,* Max thought.

"Okay, he is *so* going to pay!" Ashleigh seethed, creating her signature lightning daggers. "Let me at him!"

"Okay." Trina shrugged. "Just don't do anything stupid." Before Trina finished her sentence, Ashleigh bounded at the robber, throwing a dagger. The robber ducked under the dagger, sidestepping another swipe from Ashleigh.

"I have daggers. You don't. I have the advantage. Just give up already," Ashleigh said.

The robber chuckled, unsheathing a pair of red glowing daggers. "Who said anything about advantages?"

Ashleigh and the robber danced on the ground, blades flashing. Ashleigh moved forward to strike the robber in the gut, but he easily blocked it, kicking Ashleigh backward. *He's better than I am at using daggers,* Ashleigh thought. *Guess I'll have to even the odds.* Ashleigh got up and created a clone of herself. "Let's go with combo three," Ashleigh said, and the clone nodded.

Ashleigh bombarded the robber with volleys of thrown daggers, distracting and somewhat blinding him. The daggers also destroyed all the technology on the robber's armor, causing it to spark and sizzle. Then the clone got up close and personal, kicking the robber into the air. Then right before Ashleigh began the next part of her combo, a female voice in her head said, *Use the lightning cloak. I will help you activate it. But focus on your enemy.*

Both Ashleighs watched as yellow crackling electricity swirled around them, forming a sort of energy cover. *Now go! Fight thine enemy. Nobody calls my host "little girl" and gets away with it!* the voice said.

The Ashleigh clone threw the robber into the air, and Ashleigh dashed toward him with two daggers in hand. "Ready, Ashleigh?" Ashleigh asked as she ran.

"Ready," the clone answered, creating two daggers of her own. Ashleigh jumped into the air and slashed the man with a dagger, making a long cut on the chest part of the armor. Then her clone zoomed in, slashing the man on the arm. The pair continued like this, zigzagging across the robber. But unbeknownst to them, the lightning cloak had increased their speed, allowing them to move at eye-splitting speeds.

"So fast!" Trina remarked, astonished.

The Ashleighs were moving so fast all the kids could see were yellow streaks!

Ashleigh created another clone in midair, this one creating a ball of electricity in her hands. At first, it was only a couple inches in size, but then it turned to a couple feet. Yellow flashes circled around the robber as the Ashleighs assaulted him.

"Now!" Ashleigh yelled, and her and her first clone jumped back. They created smaller balls of electricity in their hands. Then all three Ashleighs rushed forward, slamming the electric spheres into the robber.

"Combo! Triple-shock sphere stage one!" the Ashleighs chorused as the electric spheres exploded. "That's what you get for calling me little girl!" The entire lobby was enveloped in yellow light, followed by a loud *BANG!* Then there was a quiet *thud*, and the light faded.

When the kids uncovered their eyes, they saw the robber on the ground, unconscious, with his armor in pieces on the floor around him. Ashleigh and her clones were sitting down, panting. The lightning cloaks had faded away, but the Ashleighs were grinning widely. "Feels good to let your creative side out sometimes," Ashleigh said as her clones disappeared with flashes of electricity.

Inwardly, Ashleigh said, *Thanks…whoever you are, for showing me that lightning-cloak thing.*

You're welcome, the voice said again. *And call me Vira. Also, I may be mistaken, but I think your friend Jessica has Lana.*

Who's Lana? Ashleigh asked.

She was my friend. Before we died anyway, Vira replied. *She was a water user, just like Jessica. And I'm just like you, a lightning user. You get your powers from me.*

Ashleigh's eyes widened. *Okay, hold on. Jessica and I have dead people inside of us?! That is wrong on so many levels. And if Jessica and I have dead people, do Max and Damian? And Connor? And Trina? And Ronan?*

Ashleigh could feel Vira rolling her eyes. *If my senses aren't deceiving me, I'd say that Ragnar and Crogan are inside Max and Damian respectively. And Ronan has Wyat. All five of us "dead people" are the sources of your powers. We supply you with Warrior Energy. Or more specifically,* our *Warrior Energy.*

This was a lot to take in, but Ashleigh, being Ashleigh, said, *Does this mean I have a leg up on the others? I now know more about our powers than they do!*

Vira sighed. *Trina and Max might have caught on, but otherwise, yes. You sound just like me at your age.*

Ashleigh grinned, getting to her feet. The attendant had gotten up, staring in awe at Ashleigh. And also, Ashleigh could hear the police coming. "We should probably get going," Ashleigh voiced, glancing at the door. Police vehicles were coming into the parking lot, and Ashleigh didn't want it to look like she was the bad guy.

"Thank you so much!" the attendant said gratefully. "I'll be sure to tell the police what a good job you did."

Ashleigh rubbed her neck sheepishly. "Umm, sure! Now, Trina, get us outta here!"

Trina nodded. "Since we don't have much time, I'm not going to use portals. I'll just teleport each of you onto your Starcycles."

Trina placed her hands on Max's and Damian's shoulders, and they disappeared with a *pop!* She then teleported Jessica and Ashleigh, followed by Connor and Ronan. Then with everyone gone, she gave a nod to the attendant and popped out. And they were just in time too 'cause police officers rushed into the room, laser rifles at the ready.

The kids mounted their Starcycles, pulling out of the driveway. As Max put his helmet on, he jokingly said, "Note to self: never get on Ashleigh's bad side."

"Right," Ashleigh said. "And, Trina?"

"Yeah?" Trina responded.

"When we get back, can you check our minds? There's this voice I keep hearing inside my head," Ashleigh said.

Trina shrugged, though she was a bit concerned about that. "Okay."

Really! Vira fumed. *You've been hearing voices in your head? Really!*

Ashleigh laughed, grinning at her own antics. *What?* Ashleigh asked innocently. *For all I know, you don't exist, and I'm just hearing voices.*

Vira growled angrily, but then remained silent. She'd have her revenge.

Meanwhile, the others looked at Ashleigh worriedly. "What's she laughing at?" Damian asked. The others shrugged.

The kids weaved through the streets, evading traffic and heading toward their base. As they spotted their tower, they switched to flight mode, lifting into the air. They zipped across the water, floating into the entrance of the base. The kids dropped to the ground, parking. As they removed their helmets, Trina said, "All right, come here, Ashleigh."

Ashleigh removed her helmet and walked over to Trina. Trina placed her hands on Ashleigh's head, entering her mind.

Trina appeared in a vast white place. As she looked around, she saw Ashleigh standing a few meters beside her. Beside Ashleigh was another figure about a foot taller. She was female, with dirty-blonde hair. "Looks like Ashleigh isn't the only one in her head," Trina muttered to herself.

She then walked toward Ashleigh and the other figure. "Hey, Ashleigh," Trina said friendlily. "Who's that beside you?"

The figure responded before Ashleigh could, "I'm Vira, this small brat's source of energy. I'm the one that gives her, her powers."

"I'm not a brat!" Ashleigh pouted.

"Oh." Trina was more than a little bit surprised at the information. "If you are the source of Ashleigh's powers, do all the others have someone like you inside them?" Trina asked.

"Yes," Vira said. "All your friends have my friends inside of them."

"How'd you even get inside Ashleigh?" Trina wondered aloud.

"Well, I died. Then with my last dying breath, I decided to give my life force, my Warrior Energy, to someone who would carry on my will. Though how I got stuck with a kid puzzles me," Vira said.

"So we have dead people inside of us?" Trina asked.

"How come you kids keep saying that?" Vira asked exasperatedly. "But yes."

Okay," Trina said. "I'm just gonna leave now."

Trina exited Ashleigh's mind, going back to the world of the living. "So either Ashleigh really has another entity inside her, or the two of us are going crazy. And according to that other entity, Vira, you guys have people inside of you too," Trina said.

Several jaws dropped. But Max wasn't fazed. "I figured as much. At least, from what that Ignisean Elder told me. What's the name of the one inside of me?"

Ragnar, answered a voice from inside him.

Nice, Max said. *That's a pretty awesome name.*

"What's mine?" Damian asked.

Crogan, a voice said from inside Damian.

Sick name, Damian said with a grin.

"What about mine?" Jessica asked.

Lana, answered a voice from inside her.

That's a pretty name, Jessica complimented.

"Mine?" Ronan asked.

Wyat, answered a voice.

116

Nice, Ronan said.

"What about mine?" Trina asked.

"You don't have one since you were born with your powers. And neither does Connor," Ashleigh answered.

"Aww." Trina groaned dejectedly. "Wait a minute! How'd you know I was born with my powers?"

Ashleigh shrugged. "Vira told me."

"That is seriously creepy," Trina said.

"So let me get this straight," Ronan said. "We have *energy beings* inside us?"

Ashleigh nodded. "Pretty much!"

"And they can speak to us in our minds."

"Yep."

"Awesome!"

"Also," Ashleigh said, "they can show you things about your powers since they are actually theirs."

Wyat? Ronan asked.

Okay, Wyat answered, knowing what Ronan was about to ask.

Ronan walked upstairs, Wyat teaching him new things about his powers.

You up for a lesson, kid? Ragnar asked.

You've been with me for something like a week. What do you think? Max responded.

Great! Ragnar said enthusiastically. *So you can create constructs to act on your behalf…*

C'mon, Lana, Jessica said, walking after Ronan and Max.

"I have a feeling that those guys are not gonna get any sleep tonight," Trina said. "And speaking of which, it's still daytime. Wanna spar?" she asked Connor.

Connor nodded, and the two walked off to another room. Ashleigh and Damian walked up to the room, wanting to join the others. But they were surprised to find them collapsed on their beds, exhausted.

"If you can't beat 'em, join 'em!" Ashleigh said, dropping onto her bed.

Damian followed suit, falling asleep only minutes later.

CHAPTER 14

Ragnar Is the Best Name—Deal with It

Max was the first to rise, rubbing his eyes and yawning. *Boy, do I feel refreshed!* he thought to himself.

Maybe that has to do with the fact that you slept for almost twelve hours, Ragnar said.

Did I really sleep that long? Max asked as he got out of his bed.

Yes.

Max quietly opened the door, slipping out of the room. *How about a quick training session?*

What do I have to lose?

Your fate has been decided, Max joked, getting a snort from Ragnar.

Max walked into the main room, still marveling at the technology. But he passed the large area, walking into another room. It was a very long space, about thirty meters long and ten meters wide.

Ready, old man? Max asked.

Do you want to die early? Ragnar asked sourly.

I've come close to death before. And also, you really can't do anything to me. You don't control my powers.

To a little extent, yes. I can make one of your powers activate if you're in danger. But I can't put you in danger myself. Like how Vira activated the lightning cloak for Ashleigh while she was fighting.

Good to know, Ragnar, Max said.

Oh, and since you're by yourself, you're going to want a clone to spar with, Ragnar suggested.

How do I make a clone? Max asked.

Look at where you want the clone to appear. Then imagine yourself in that spot. Now shape it with your fire and—boom!—you have a clone. As you keep using the ability, you won't have to take that much time to do it, as shown with Ashleigh, Ragnar guided.

Max nodded, raising his arms. He outlined himself in the space beside him, fire crackling in the air. Then Max poured fire into that shape, using his raw Warrior Energy to make it exactly like himself. After a few seconds of energy outpour, Max stopped, staring at the spot. It was like he was looking into a mirror. Another Max stood right in front of him, grinning.

"So you wanted to spar?" the clone asked.

Max nodded, gaining a grin of his own. The clone attacked without warning, coating his right fist in flames as he struck. Max dodged the blow, jumping backward. Max fashioned a fire sword, twirling the blade in the air. "Let's go wild," he said, and the clone grinned even wider.

Don't go too wild, Ragnar said cautiously. *Wouldn't want to destroy this place, now would you?*

Flames enveloped both Max and his clone, increasing the heat. *Can we do something like Ashleigh's lightning cloak? Except with fire?* Max asked Ragnar.

Does that seem hard to do?

From inside Max, Ragnar curled and twisted the flames around Max until they formed something like an exoskeleton. The flames followed Max's contour, making a perfect outer skin. "Time to play," Max said, cracking his inflamed knuckles.

Without a word, Max shot forward, slamming his fist into his clone's gut. The clone flew back several meters, wiping dirt from his mouth but was otherwise unharmed. Max didn't waste time, throwing a giant fireball at the clone. As the fireball hit its mark, it started to shrink, dissipating completely after about a second. But when the fireball disappeared, the clone wasn't there. *Now where could he—*

Behind you! Ragnar alerted, cutting Max off. Max ducked under a kick from his clone, grabbing the leg. He then threw his clone into the air, shooting a fireball after him. The clone dodged the fireball, landing on the ground ten meters away. The clone then rushed toward Max, raising his fists. Max threw several fireballs in quick succession, hoping to hit the clone at least once.

I don't even think I can call that a strategy, Ragnar commented.

Max huffed. *If I remember correctly, I'm fighting myself. He has the same brain as me. I need to be unpredictable.*

Well, now I know you aren't completely hopeless, Ragnar said.

Max didn't respond, continuing his fireball assault. The clone effortlessly evaded the fireballs, only absorbing them when they got too close for comfort. The clone quickly closed in, throwing a punch. Max caught it with his hand, but wasn't quick enough to evade a knee to the groin. Max's eyes widened, and he fell backward, groaning in pain.

Ragnar hummed in approval. *A blow to the family jewels. That always gets them.*

"My clone is too good," Max muttered, getting to his feet. His clone was already running at him. *Ragnar, prepare to witness an awesome maneuver.*

The clone threw a punch, but Max arched his back backward so that he could see his clone's fist. Then Max kicked the clone into the air with his left foot, balancing all of his weight on his right leg. Max placed his foot back on the ground, jumping into the air. He grabbed the clone by the leg, throwing him higher into the air.

Max then brought his heel down on the clone's stomach, sending the clone shooting down to the ground. But Max wasn't done yet. Max pyro-ported below the clone, raising his sword to plunge it into the clone's head. But the sword never touched skin.

Max looked up at his sword to see orange fiery tendrils holding it down. "Aargh!" he cried out in frustration.

Don't lose your cool, Ragnar said. *You can beat him. Just think. Hard. You yourself said before that in order to beat yourself, you have to be unpredictable. Now normally, what would you do in this situation?*

Max thought hard. *I'd pyro-port behind my enemy to escape.*

Exactly, Ragnar said. *Your clone would expect you to do this. Now what would he not expect you to do?*

It finally clicked in Max's head. *This.*

Max let go of his sword, spinning around. He slammed his fist into his clone's jaw, sending him flying. He followed the punch up with a fireball, launching it at the clone. *Now he's going to pyro-port behind me.*

Max turned around, and sure enough, his clone was behind him, wiping blood from his mouth. The clone threw a fireball at Max, but he absorbed it with his hand, shooting one back at the clone. The clone stretched out his hand to absorb the flames, but stopped when Max's fist slammed into his chin.

The clone fell backward, landing on his back. But then the clone pyro-ported away, appearing twenty meters away from Max. The clone then created two fire swords, rushing toward Max. *Okay, this just became dangerous*, Max thought.

Oh, please, Ragnar said. *I've dealt with worse.*

Ignoring Ragnar's comment, Max outstretched his hands. Two fiery tendrils erupted from the ground in front of him. "I need *way* more than that," Max said to himself, moving his arms in different directions. Several more tendrils appeared across the space, going from tens to hundreds. The clone simply waved his swords, cutting down any tendrils in the way.

"Here goes nothing!" Max said, raising his arms. All the tendrils elongated, shooting toward the clone. Two of the tendrils went for the swords, wrapping around the flaming blades. Ten of the tendrils wrapped around the clone's arms and legs, keeping him from moving. Then the remainder of the tendrils snaked across his stomach and chest, only stopping at the clone's neck. The tendrils then lifted the clone into the air, and Max grabbed his sword out of the ground, running at his doppelganger. The clone couldn't move, but his eyes widened in fear as Max pulled his sword to the side, running straight past the clone.

A couple seconds passed, and nothing happened. Then the clone's head hit the ground with a soft thud, disappearing with a burst of flame. "Dang," Max heard a voice say from behind him.

Battle instincts kicked in; Max threw his sword horizontally at the figure.

"Woah!" Damian said as he jumped away from the flaming sword. "You don't have to kill me for simply speaking!"

"Sorry," Max apologized, the fire cloak dissipating. "I was battle-ready, you know?"

Damian waved his apology aside. "I get it. Looks like you had fun, though."

"Nah. It was rather boring. It only went on for as long as it did because I wanted to test out new abilities," Max said.

That is most definitely not true, Ragnar said crossly. *You asked for my help several times, yet you still struggled.*

After a moment of staring at Max, Damian said, "Liar. Even *you* aren't that good."

I like this kid. Maybe I should have gone to him and not you, Ragnar sniped.

You have mortally wounded me, Ragnar, Max said.

My pleasure.

"Anyway," Damian continued, "come on! Everyone's awake, and there are things we have to discuss."

Max shook his head. "I'd rather be training right now."

I thought so, Damian thought. *I must pull out my trump card.* "Also, breakfast is ready. We're having scrambled eggs with pancakes. I hope they haven't finished eating it by now."

Max's eyes widened, and Damian sweat-dropped. "Nooo! The food of the gods must not be finished. I must consume it!" With that, Max dashed out of the training room, the smell of pancakes and scrambled eggs making him realize just how hungry he was.

Why do I get stuck with the idiot? Ragnar wondered.

Max sprinted into the main room, seeing everyone already eating. "Nooo!" he cried. "The food of the gods must not be finished!"

The kids all stared at him like he was off his rocker. "Are you good?" Trina asked as she swallowed a spoonful of scrambled eggs.

Max regained his composure. "Yes, of course."

Inside Ashleigh, Vira chuckled quietly. *My nonexistent heart bleeds for you, Ragnar.*

Max grabbed a plate, taking two pancakes. He then shoved more than ten spoonfuls of scrambled eggs into his plate, licking his lips. "This," he said between a mouthful of scrambled eggs, "is good. Who made it?"

"We did!" Damian, Jessica, Ronan, and Trina chorused.

"Damian and Jessica made the pancakes," Ronan said.

"And Ronan and I made the scrambled eggs," Trina answered cheerily.

"How'd you even make that stuff without a frying pan or a stove? Where'd you even get eggs? Or flour? Or milk? Or sugar?" Max asked.

"I bought the ingredients. I also created the frying pan and stove," Trina said. Then she stared blankly into the space in front of her. "I haven't cooked in such a long time...," she mused. Then she pulled her knees to herself and began rocking back and forth.

Ashleigh waved her hand in front of Trina's face. "Hello? Earth to Trina?"

Trina didn't respond.

Fine, Ashleigh thought. "We're being attacked! Ronan just got hit! Man down, man down! It looks like it's fatal!"

Trina snapped out of her daze, jumping to her feet with her sword at the ready. Her hair floated around her as she raged. "I will smite you puny mortals for harming my brother! Have at thee!"

Ashleigh choked on her scrambled eggs, rolling on the ground, laughing. "Oh, man!" She laughed. "Everyone's so out of it today!"

Max finished his scrambled eggs, taking a bite out of his first pancake. His taste buds practically exploded with pleasure! The pancakes tasted so good! "Woah," he whispered. "Even though these two are my favorite foods, I've never tasted anything as sweet as it! What did you use!"

The pancakes were light and fluffy, practically melting in Max's mouth. "Normal pancake batter," Jessica said, "but instead of sugar, Damian and I used a plant called a mayan mint. It's said to be one thousand times sweeter than sugar, so we gave it a go."

Max made a mental note to tell his mom to use mayan mints instead of sugar. He quickly finished his pancakes, though, ready for another sparring match. But before he could even open his mouth, a bright spiraling shape appeared beside him. Air spewed out of it with the sound of a jet engine, almost blowing Max away. But then an object shot out of the white space, crashing into Max and closing the shape.

Max blinked several times, trying to figure out what on earth had just happened. He could feel something on top of him, but he was too dazed to try and get it off. Then the object groaned, rolling off Max. "Oww," the figure muttered, rubbing its head. "I need to get better with that."

Then Max glanced at the figure, his brain fully functional now. It was a girl his age, from the looks of it, a couple inches taller than him. Her hair was a reddish-brown color and stretched to the middle of her back. Her skin was a light-tan color, and her eyes were hazel.

The girl got to her feet, stretching her arms, but the rest of the team was in position to strike at any second. Before the girl could register what was happening, green vines wrapped around her arms and legs, restraining her. "Who are you?" Connor asked, keeping the vines steady.

The girl frowned, saying, "I'm Emily. And you guys are?"

"That's not important," Connor said.

"Why are you here?" Ashleigh asked, the two lightning daggers in her hands sparking.

"I would answer your question, but you look hostile," Emily said calmly.

Ashleigh hissed, throwing a dagger in frustration. Emily's calm look didn't leave her face as the dagger flew straight at her exposed head. The dagger was only a foot away from Emily's head when it stopped. It just froze, unmoving. Then the dagger shook, twisting and shooting back at Ashleigh's arm.

A gust of wind pushed the dagger away, sending it clattering to the ground before it disappeared with a burst of electricity. Ashleigh's eyes darted to Trina. "Why'd you send it back at me?"

Trina looked offended. "That wasn't me, Ashleigh."

"She's right, Ashleigh. That was me," Emily said. "For people who seem to have fought before, you sure don't seem to check your opponent's abilities before you attack them. What you saw there was my gravity manipulation. Now could you let me out?"

"Gravity manipulation, huh? How good are you?" Trina asked.

"Let's just say that if I wanted you dead, I could stick a black hole on you," Emily said.

Trina raised her eyebrows. Emily then glanced at the vines, and they flew off her, landing on the ground with a soft *thump!*

"You don't seem like a terrible person. But just to be safe, I'm going to peer into your mind and check for any malicious intent," Trina stated.

Emily shrugged, saying, "Whatever."

Trina skimmed through Emily's family memories, taking note of every important event. As she moved to the more recent ones, she saw darker, scarier memories, like ones where the Ne'faro chased her for several miles, wanting to use her for their evil cause. But despite all this, it only made Emily determined to be the best she could be. Trina couldn't find a hint of malicious intent in Emily.

Trina pulled out of Emily's mind, saying, "You pass." Then Trina decided to use the Ne'faro to her advantage. "You remember those blue-skinned creeps that followed you recently?"

"Yeah, why? You affiliated with them?" Emily slipped into a subtle defensive stance, though it was noticeable to the others.

"We aren't in league with them. In fact, we hate them more than you do, what with the fact that they captured us several times and attacked us several more for our powers," Trina explained.

Emily's eyes widened, and she said, "Here I was, thinking I was the only superpowered kid being chased by a bunch of make-up-skinned creeps."

Ashleigh snorted at the comment, saying, "You're on the team."

"Oh, so I just went through initiation?" Emily asked.

Ashleigh grinned. "But first let's have you spar with one of us," Ashleigh said. "Trina, you up for the challenge?"

Trina shook her head. "Max seems to want to do that."

Max frowned. "How'd you—"

"Mind reading."

Max shrugged, leading Emily to the training room. "So what was that thing you did there when you opened that white space and then shot out of it?" Max asked.

"You know how black holes suck things in?"

Max nodded.

"My white holes shoot things out, or at least anything that goes into the other end of it," Emily explained.

Max chuckled. "You should join NASA. They need your help traveling through space."

Emily snorted. "And there's a crazy thought."

The two entered the training room, taking separate sides of the long space.

"Ready?" Max asked.

"I was about to ask you the same thing," Emily said.

"All right, let's do this!"

Max rushed at Emily, creating a fireball in his hands. He launched the flaming sphere at Emily, creating his fire sword right after. But right before the fireball slammed into Emily, it stopped, turning back around and shooting at Max. *Right, gravity manipulation*, Max thought. *Attacks like that won't even touch her.*

Max jumped forward, slashing at Emily with his sword. Emily created a sword of her own a split second before Max's collided with her, blocking the hit. Emily jumped back, outstretching her hands. The space in front of Max distorted, and Emily threw her sword. The sword flew point first at Max's stomach, slicing through the air with a whistling sound. Alarmed, Max pyro-ported behind Emily, swinging his fist. But the sword curved the air back at Max, unrelenting.

What do I do now? Max asked Ragnar.

Make fire clones and let them take the blows for you.

Nodding to himself, Max formed five fire clones around him as the sword closed in. One clone jumped in the way of the blade as Max mixed with the rest of his clones, each of them jumping in a different direction. Max jumped into the air, creating dozens of fire shurikens in his hands. He launched them all at once, bombarding Emily with spinning fire blades. Emily outstretched her arms, blowing the weapons away. She then pointed at Max, motioning for him to move toward her. The force of gravity yanked Max out of the air, pulling him toward Emily.

Oh no, he thought. *I'm gonna die.*

Emily pulled her sword back into her free hand, plunging it into Max's stomach. But then the Max disappeared with a burst of fire, scorching Emily's arm. The real Max appeared behind Emily, kicking her into the air.

Nice maneuver, Ragnar said to Max.

Thanks, Max replied.

Emily landed on the ground, moving backward a bit. "How'd you do that?" she asked.

"It's simple, really," Max said. "When I created my five clones, while one took the blade for me, me and my remaining clones mixed up and then spread out. The 'Max' that threw the shurikens was a clone, and when you 'killed' him, he burned you when he disappeared. But right now, there are three other clones around you, including me. So you might want to watch your back."

Emily turned around just as a clone launched a giant fireball at her, increasing the temperature by Emily by hundreds of degrees. Emily ducked under the fireball, running forward toward the clone. The clone created a fire sword in his right hand, moving toward Emily as well. Emily then raised her arms, then dropped them to her sides. The clone stopped moving, gravity now tripling on it. It staggered, collapsing under its own weight. The clone then disappeared with a burst of fire.

Emily spun around, plunging her sword into the heart of another clone. She quickly jumped back before the clone burned her, glancing at another clone running toward her. Emily dropped her sword, cupping her hands. A small black orb the size of a quarter appeared in between her palms. Then the orb doubled in size, pulling anything within a ten-foot radius around it. Emily gritted her teeth, sweat flowing down her face in small beads. *C'mon*, Emily thought. *I can control this black hole.*

The clone's eyes widened as he saw the black hole, and he created two fire swords. He stuck them into the ground to give him a good grip as the black hole tugged at him. At first he was doing pretty good, but then his swords were sucked into the black hole. The black hole's imaginary arms grabbed the clone's legs, trying to suck him in. The clone was stretched out into thin human spaghetti as it was sucked in. Emily promptly closed the black hole, panting. *If I had gone any longer, I probably would've lost control,* she thought.

"So," Max said from behind her, "you defeated all of my clones. But you look very tired after using that black hole."

Emily said nothing, gasping for air. Max took a step toward her, and Emily whipped around, hair flying. She outstretched her right arm, and Max was blown backward into the wall, falling to the ground with a soft *thud.* Emily dropped do her knees, panting. She coughed several times as her lungs began to fill with air once more.

"Don't overexert yourself," Max said as he got to his feet.

Max pyro-ported to Emily, helping her up. Max then pyro-ported them into the main room, where he heard the rest of his teammates arguing over which of their dead beings had the best name.

"Obviously Vira," Ashleigh said.

"Nope!" Ronan yelled. "Wyat is clearly the best."

Max rolled his eyes. "Children, please!" Everyone turned to him. "Ragnar is the best name. Deal with it."

The others glared daggers at him, but then Trina got an idea. "Why don't we have a contest to see who's better? Race you!"

With that, the kids all took off into the training room, ready to prove their superiority.

128

Chapter 15

Let's Go Prepare the Universe for Destruction!

"We're going to do this like a battle royale," Trina explained as they dashed into the arena. "The match ends when there's only one player remaining. No more rules. Let's do this!"

"I'll be ref," Emily offered. "I just had a sparring match with Max anyway."

The kids each took spots on the space, spreading out from one another. "All right!" Emily said.

Ronan formed a wind bow in his hands, an arrow already strung. "Ready!"

Ashleigh created twin lightning daggers.

"Set!"

Trina's swords appeared in her hands.

"Go!"

The kids took off, determined to win. But Ronan stayed back, knowing that he could fight long range. *Wyat?* Ronan asked his partner.

In order to hit all of them accurately, you're going to need to shoot from the air, Wyat said. Ronan did as Wyat said, rising into the air. He scanned the area, looking for easy targets. Luckily, all the kids were preoccupied fighting one another, too distracted to notice.

Trina's going to be a major threat later, Ronan thought as he nocked an arrow. *Sorry, sis.* Ronan fired the arrow, nocking another one. The arrow flew straight at Trina's head, whizzing through the air with a sharp hissing sound.

Trina slashed at Max with her sword, but he blocked it with his own, grinning. All of a sudden, Trina got a weird feeling in her head, like there was danger nearby. Acting on instinct, Trina ducked, and a gray arrow shot past her, lodging itself in the ground. Trina raised her head, glancing in the direction the arrow came from. Sure enough, Ronan was in the air with a bow and arrow, raining death upon the kids on the ground.

Trina teleported behind Ronan, swinging her sword, but all of a sudden, he disappeared. A gust of wind slammed into Trina's chest, sending her flying into the wall. Ronan then reappeared about twenty meters away from Trina, nocking three arrows. He let them loose at his sister, but she teleported away, evading the arrows.

Ronan turned around just in time to see Trina shooting toward him, swords pressed into a point. Ronan quickly turned into air, curving around the blades. He reappeared behind Trina, firing a wind arrow. The arrow shot straight through Trina, sucking out all the air in her lungs before disappearing with a small gust of wind. Trina faltered, eyes wide, and went spiraling down to the ground, defeated.

Meanwhile, Ashleigh spun and twirled around, blades slicing through the air. Jessica used two whips to try and hit Ashleigh, sending them flying through the air, but Ashleigh cut through the whips like a knife through butter. Jessica created two new whips, rushing forward. Ashleigh's lightning cloak appeared around her, buzzing with energy. She readied her daggers, preparing for Jessica's attack.

Jessica wrapped her whips around Ashleigh, pulling it tight. *Got her now*, she thought. But Ashleigh simply grinned, increasing her energy output. The vibrations from her lightning cloak disrupted the steady flow of the water whips, causing ripples to move about in every part of the whips. The water whips then separated, dropping onto the ground and forming puddles. Jessica grunted in frustration.

Water whips are now ineffective, she thought. *I need to try something new. Lana?*

Puddle trap, Lana suggested.

And that is?

Let me help you.

The two puddles from the water whips grew, spreading around Ashleigh. Ripples pulsed throughout the water as Ashleigh's lightning cloak hummed. Ashleigh thought nothing of it, contemplating what she should do next. She shifted her footing, preparing to launch herself at Jessica. *With the speed at which I'd be going, Jessica won't even know what hit her*, she thought.

Ashleigh darted forward, but right as she moved, two water chains grabbed her ankles, pulling her to the ground. *What?* Ashleigh thought. The chains dragged her across the ground toward the puddle as the kicked and flailed, desperately trying to escape.

What do I do? Ashleigh asked Vira.

Well, if I'd known it was the puddle trap before, I'd have warned you. But at this point, all you can do is hold your breath and hope you are pulled out before you drown, Vira advised her.

Wait, drown?

Yep. Lana's puddle trap makes a small puddle, then sort of increases the depth of it by who knows what.

Ashleigh panicked, trying to figure out a way to escape. She then noticed her daggers. *Aha!* she thought. She sliced through one of the chains with her dagger, twisting around to cut the other one. But then another chain wrapped around her leg, pulling her even harder. She took a deep breath as she was yanked into the water.

Will that kill her? Jessica asked Lana.

Only if you want it to, Lana replied.

Ashleigh stayed perfectly still underneath the surface, wanting to save her air. From what she could feel, the chains were still dragging her farther down, however slowly. *I can't stay here forever, and Jessica knows that*, she thought. But she was inevitably using up her air, and she couldn't go on so much longer.

Will flying out of here work? Ashleigh asked Vira.

You're already in the water. At this point, you're completely at Jessica's mercy.

Ashleigh then ran out of air, and she began struggling again, wiggling around. *I'm gonna die! I'm gonna die!* she thought frantically. But then the chains stopped pulling her down. They then turned upward, pulling her up three times faster than they went down. Water rushed past Ashleigh as her face slowly started to turn a pale blue. But she erupted from the water just in time, gasping for air as she landed on her knees. When she could speak, she only said two words: "I yield."

Jessica grinned but was worried for her nearly drowned friend. *She'll be fine*, Lana said.

At the same time, Max and Damian took on Connor and Ronan, working together almost as well as Max did with Ashleigh. Damian blocked another wind arrow with his ice shield, slashing at Connor with his sword. The four had been going for a while, but neither could seem to land a solid blow on the other.

Why don't you use the exploding glacier combo? Crogan suggested. *Ragnar and I used to use it all the time on enemies. It was our signature move!*

I don't suppose you're going to tell me what it is, Damian thought.

Just tell Max that I said to use the exploding glacier combo. Ragnar will help him out, and I you.

Damian nodded, calling to Max. "Crogan wanted us to use the exploding glacier combo," he explained.

Ooh! Ragnar said from inside Max. *Our signature! Let me help you.*

Damian moved backward as Max created four fire clones. The clones rushed at Connor and Ronan, bombarding them with glowing punches and kicks. But their main job was to distract the two while Damian worked his magic. Damian outstretched both arms and fired two beams of ice at Connor and Ronan. The clones jumped out of the way as ice surrounded the two.

"Your clones landed the necessary hits, right?" Damian asked.

Max nodded, grinning as his clones disappeared. "Now I just need to coat the outside."

Max launched himself forward, creating his fire cloak to boost his speed. He landed quick glowing blows to the ice around Ronan and Connor, making the ice glow orange from the inside out. His fists and feet moved faster than any eyes could follow, not missing any spots on the ice. He then jumped off the ice, moving back. "Now!" Damian shouted.

Max clenched his fists, and all the glowing marks exploded, both on the inside and the outside. The ice shattered completely, shards flying everywhere. Connor and Ronan still stood, though unmoving. But then the two staggered, falling forward onto their faces, unconscious. Max and Damian high-fived, turning around to face Jessica.

"So we're the last ones standing, huh?" Jessica said.

Max and Damian nodded. "Let's get to it."

The two boys rushed Jessica, swords at the ready. Jessica stood her ground, readying her whips. Max threw a dozen fire shurikens, creating a clone. Jessica jumped into the air to dodge them, but Max threw another dozen at her, giving her no way out. Or so Max thought. Jessica's eyes quickly scanned her surroundings, looking for a way to evade them. A shuriken flew at her head, but she banked, dodging the flying projectile.

Another one raced at her arm, but she whipped it aside with her water whip, steam rising from the spot. Then Jessica rolled under another one, landing on the ground. She raised her right arm and wrapped her whip around Damian.

That's not going to work, Lana said.

Sure enough, the temperature within a five-foot radius of Damian dropped to zero degrees Fahrenheit. The water froze, and Damian broke through it, sending ice shards into the air. Damian raised his arms, and the shards floated in the air above him. Then he directed them at Jessica, bombarding her with sharp ice fragments.

Jessica tried her best to dodge but inevitably took some minor damage. Several cuts appeared on her skin, though they healed almost instantly given her enhanced healing. Jessica rushed forward, landing a solid kick to Damian's stomach. Damian was sent flying ten meters away, skidding as he landed on the ground. Max sent a fireball at Jessica, but she canceled it out with a giant stream of water. Steam covered the area as the two attacks stopped with a *hiss*.

All of you are pretty blind now, Lana said. *But with water powers, you're at an advantage. You can sort of sense your surroundings with all the water around you. All those tiny water droplets are technically part of you.*

Jessica closed her eyes, feeling the mist around her. She could feel the different water droplets moving around, each one doing their own thing. Jessica then felt a figure coming toward her. She raised her arms, and the mist around her curled into what looked like water tendrils. The tendrils grabbed the figure by the ankles, and he was sent waving in the air. Then all the water droplets froze, dropping to the ground. Damian wriggled out of the frozen tendrils, now able to see.

Jessica surrounded herself with water, creating a giant puddle about fifteen feet in diameter. Damian and Max came rushing into the giant puddle, unaware of Jessica's plan. The moment the boys stepped into the water, Jessica slammed her hands onto the ground, sending circular ripples throughout the puddle. The ripples then turned into swirls, pulling the water around Jessica like a vortex. The boys' eyes widened as they were pulled by the whirlpool. It only took four seconds for them to be completely submerged.

Very nice, Lana said. *You used your creativity to create something useful.*

Looks like I win, Jessica thought.

Then the whirlpool froze, creating a beautiful spiral shape. But Jessica's feet were in the water, and she was frozen from the calf down. "Nani!" she cried. Damian and Max broke through the ice, grinning widely.

"You didn't seriously think it'd be that easy to get rid of us, did you?" Max asked.

"I have no choice in the next one," Jessica said seriously. Jessica raised her arms, focusing on the boys. *The human body is made of over 60 percent water*, Jessica thought. The boys suddenly stood perfectly straight, arms at their sides.

"What's going on?" Max asked.

"I don't know," Damian said.

Jessica brought her arms together, and the boys slammed into each other. Jessica pulled her arms apart, and the boys were flung into the walls.

You're better than I was at your age, Lana complimented her. Jessica didn't respond, still focused on her opponents. Max's hands clenched into fists as he started hitting himself, wincing as he did.

If this goes on much longer, I'm going to get seriously injured, Max thought. "I yield!" he yelled.

"Same here!" Damian added.

Jessica dropped her arms, grinning. "And I win!" she said.

All the others surrounded her, smiling widely. "Nice job, Jessica," Ashleigh congratulated her.

Damian created an ice trophy, saying, "Store it in the freezer, polish it, and keep it safe. It's the only one."

"Oh, shut up!" Jessica giggled.

"All right, now that we've had our fun, we need to negotiate with all the other planets for the upcoming war," Max said. "Suit up. We're going to our home planets. Your dead companions will help you find them. As for Trina and Emily, you can just stay here and do whatever. Just don't break anything."

Emily shrugged, walking upstairs. The rest of the kids rushed downstairs into their garage, mounting their Starcycles and pulling on their helmets. With a snap of her fingers, Trina changed their outfits, teleporting back upstairs. The girls' clothing changed to white dresses, black leather jackets on top, and black knee-high wedge boots. The boys, on the other hand, got gray short-sleeved shirts and black leather jackets. They also wore black high-top sneakers. Max said over the speakers, "Let's go prepare the universe for destruction."

Max revved his Starcycle's engine and took off into the air. "We should split up," Max suggested. "It'll save us a lot of time." After a couple seconds of the kids speaking to their partners, Max grinned evilly, saying, "Now that, that's over, I call dibs on Ignis!"

Damian responded, "Glacies-9!"

Connor said, "Naturae-37!"

"Oceanum-22!" Jessica exclaimed.

"Zulcae-15!" Ashleigh beamed.

"Venta-16," Ronan offered.

Max steered his Starcycle in the direction of the Panther constellation. "Follow my lead," he said. He looked at his GPS screen. There was a blue digital button flashing. It beeped: *Do you want to activate OverDrive mode?* He clicked the button. The engine hummed, excited to be useful. They blasted off into space, shooting past different planets and stars. "Split up! Your planet should look unique—one distinctive trait," Max said. He veered his Starcycle to the left, toward Ignis.

Want to know something ironic? Flying through the vacuum of space was easy, but flying through Ignis's atmosphere was about two millimeters away from being impossible. Its atmosphere was swelteringly hot, even for Max. The heat there was so intense it made his view of his Starcycle so distorted and hard to see that he almost crashed into a random flying ship.

Max activated the shield, but it went up in flames instantly. He activated autopilot and pulled his hands off the steering wheel. He clicked both of the discs on his gloves, and they glowed blue. "Identity please," it sounded. "Maxwell Channing," Max responded. It vibrated, and metal coils snaked up his arms. The coils tightened into armor and made their way down his legs and up his face. A transparent steel mask covered the eye part of the helmet.

A heads-up display popped up on the mask. Max landed safely on the ground next to a lava pit, which shot a bunch of lava into the air about a couple feet from him. "And that," Max said aloud, "is about as safe as you can be here."

The elder he'd seen only a day and a half ago rose slowly from the pit. His eyes were closed, but deep inside, Max knew he could sense him anyway. When the elder spoke, his voice was deep and gravelly. "You came to speak to us?" He opened his eyes, which seemed to be debating whether to be carrot orange or ruby red.

Max cracked a small smile. "In case you didn't notice, to us earthlings, having another completely different race tell you something they shouldn't have known unless you told them is horrifying."

The elder rubbed his chin in consideration.

"But that's not the point," Max said quickly.

"Follow me," the elder said. "You are immune to lava, right?" he inquired.

"Pretty much," Max replied. The elder jumped into one of the lava pits, and Max said, "That doesn't look good for my health." Nevertheless, he jumped. When they landed, they trekked up a spiraling staircase into a large space. It was around sixty feet straight across and forty feet from side to side. Just as Max stepped into the edge, he was knee-deep in lava.

They waded five feet farther. By then, Max was waist-deep. Something made a large ripple in the lava, and Max felt something scaly rub against his leg. He ignored it but saw a black spiny object undulate only meters in front of him. "Uh, Elder, is this place sa—"

A large black dragon-like monster raised itself out of the lava pool. It roared and studied Max carefully. He made the mistake of moving his right hand, and it lunged.

CHAPTER 16

The Moment Max Realized Everything in *How to Train Your Dragon* Was Not a Lie

A few years ago, if someone told Jessica, "Hey, I flew to another planet that habits life on an alien hovercycle!" she wouldn't have believed them. Nowadays, it was like, "Been there, done that." But now Jessica was rocketing through space at millions of miles an hour. If it wasn't for her helmet, her face would have peeled off three million meters ago. Then she spotted a blue glowing planet in the distance. *Water!* she thought joyfully.

Oceanum! Lana rejoiced, glad to see her home planet. Jessica entered its atmosphere only seconds later.

As Jessica sliced through the planet's protective layer, she felt invigorated. Water droplets gathered on her jacket, and the rest turned to mist as she cut through it like a knife. She was unprepared when she crashed into the ocean.

Please tell me there's a submarine mode on this thing, Jessica thought. As if on cue, the Starcycle turned into a subcycle: steering wheel, closed space, and moving through water. Jessica turned off the Starcycle and pocketed the activation whistle the archers had given each of them. She removed her helmet, opened the hatch, and swam out into the water. She felt stronger there—more at home.

A few Oceani swam over to greet Jessica. Others glared at her in distaste. But hey, haters gonna hate. The girls swam around Jessica, trying to study her. She swam toward a strip of land, and they followed her, giggling. Jessica climbed onto the land and found paradise. It was sunny, and there were fragrant fruits on trees blossoming everywhere.

As Jessica studied her surroundings, she noticed a tan blur dash past her. She followed its faint scent of strawberries and ended up in a flower patch. She just wanted to lie there and sleep—not a care in the world. But she shook her head and cleared her thoughts. She had a job to do.

"So you found me," a sneering male voice echoed through the air.

"Who are you? Show yourself," Jessica demanded.

A shadow moved in front of her. In its place stood a teenage boy with tan skin, blond hair, and piercing blue eyes. "Show myself? My true form or me as I am now?" His voice was as soft as silk yet cold and hard as steel.

"What? I don't understand. Well, either I don't understand, or that statement was just dumb," Jessica said.

"Puny humans," the boy said. A gust of wind blew.

A couple seconds passed, and Jessica yawned. "Are you going to try to kill me or what? That's what you're here for, right?"

The boy shrugged. "Those were my orders. But it's going to be way too easy to kill a pathetic little thing like—"

Before the boy could finish, Jessica slammed her fist into his cheek, sending him skidding across the grass. Tiny pebbles scraped his face and arms, giving him tiny cuts.

"You were saying something about how it'd be too easy to kill me, right?" Jessica asked, staring at her knuckle.

The boy stood up, spitting sand out of his mouth. He then roared in anger. His fingernails extended into talons, and his face extended into a snout with long slits for eyes. He grew enormous wings and a spiky tail. In place of the boy, a black twenty-foot-long dragon stood, its ugly head reared. The dragon growled and lunged at Jessica, its black talons gleaming.

Jessica jumped to the side, pulling water from the ocean near her. She sent a giant stream of water at the dragon, pushing it away. But then it flapped its wings, sending a powerful gust of wind toward Jessica. The water stream was diverted, and Jessica was thrown into a nearby tree. She groaned in pain but quickly got up, realizing that her fight wasn't over.

Glancing at the ocean, Jessica looked at the dragon, which was sniffing the air to find her. *So it can't see me right now*, Jessica noted. Stealthy and quick as a cat burglar, Jessica snuck toward the ocean, glancing at the dragon every now and then. It sniffed the air and stopped, turning toward Jessica. It quickly bounded after her, but it was too late. Jessica jumped into the water and disappeared under the surface. *Ha*, she thought, *that stupid dragon can't follow me now.* But then the dragon plunged into the water after Jessica. *Nani!*

The dragon's features changed. Its snout stayed, but it grew two horns on either side of its head. Its hind legs turned into tentacles with hooks on the inside. The ends of its seven tentacles were pointed and curved. It had sharp teeth, and its skin was tinged aqua green. It had two front arms that hosted five deadly claws. It was now about thirty feet in length—and enraged.

Jessica's eyes widened, and she turned away, swimming for her life. The dragon gave chase and quickly gained on her. Jessica couldn't fight it with force. Outswimming it wouldn't work either. That left distraction and wits. Jessica gave a burst of speed and pulled ahead. She then moved her arms in circular motions, creating a ring of whirlpools around her. She rose out of the water, and the tides went haywire. Giant waves crashed against the sand, and storm clouds gathered in the sky. It began to rain torrentially, and the droplets splashed on Jessica's skin, calming her.

But before Jessica reached mental equilibrium, the moody teenage dragon shot out of the water, wrapping its tentacles around Jessica. The sharp hooks cut Jessica's skin, causing blood to drip from her arms and legs. *Dang it, dang it, dang it! I done screwed up!* Jessica thought. Jessica nearly passed out in terror as the dragon pulled Jessica toward its mouth.

* * * * *

Max shoved the elder out of the way as the monster bit the empty air beside them. The monster was scaly, with sharp black spines down its back. When its tail flicked up, Max saw five spikes aligned on each side: left, right, front, back, and on the tip of the tail. Its mouth was lined with rows of rotating teeth.

It made a gurgling sound, and its eye slits narrowed. It spat lava at the elder, but he absorbed it with his hand, launching it back at the monster. The elder's hand glowed orange, and fireballs rained from above the monster. It hissed and retreated under the lava. Max and the elder stood back to back, watching out for any ripples in the lava lake. Max then spotted the monster's black spines in front of him, and he created a fireball in his hands. The monster shot out of the lava, arching in the air toward Max. It opened its mouth, roaring triumphantly. But Max then launched the fireball at the monster's eye. The flames didn't do much damage but left the monster irritated.

The monster ducked back under the lava, resting until it found a time to strike.

I wonder if I can control lava, Max thought. *It seems more or less the same as controlling fire.*

You should be able to, Ragnar said. *I mean, I could when I was alive.*

Max outstretched his arms, watching the lava. He tugged at the hot liquidy substance, trying to get a feel of it. The lava didn't respond. "C'mon," Max encouraged, trying again. This time, the lava bubbled but, otherwise, didn't do anything.

"One more time," Max muttered. He tried again, this time pulling with more force. A small stream of lava curled into the air, following Max's hands as he twisted it.

"Good," the elder smiled. "You're getting it."

The monster lurched out of the pool again, aiming at the elder. But this time, Max was ready. Rotating his arms, he made the lava around the monster form a whirlpool, keeping the monster from regaining its balance. The elder jumped forward, landing a glowing punch to the monster's stomach. An orange glowing mark grew brighter before exploding and sending the monster right back into the lava.

Max then created his fire sword, letting the flames lick the air. As the monster rose out of the lava once more, Max enlarged the sword, going from about three feet in length to ten. Max jumped forward, swinging the sword. It sliced across the monster's neck, severing its head from its body. The monster fell into the lava lifelessly, burning away as its life force faded.

"That was a unique experience," Max muttered, letting his sword disappear. "Let's continue."

Max and the elder moved through the hot lava and soon arrived at a black obsidian door. The elder placed his hand on the door, and it glowed bright orange, unlocking with a loud *click!* The two walked into a very wide room, about forty feet in length. There were thirty elders sitting on the ground, conversing quietly.

Ragnar? Max thought to his companion.

No, Ragnar said, knowing fully well what Max was about to ask.

Please? I'm no good with diplomacy. Plus, you were born here, and they all know you.

Nope.

I'll sick Jessica and Lana on you.

Noo! Not the puddle trap! Anything but that! Fine, you win!

Ha!

Max created a fire clone, but this time not of himself but of Ragnar. He imagined his chiseled features in his head, incorporating it into the clone. By the time he was done, you wouldn't be able to tell the difference between the real Ragnar and the clone. The manifestation of Ragnar cleared his throat. All the elders in the room hushed, watching him.

"Ragnar?" one asked. "I thought you died."

"I did," Ragnar replied. "But then I jumped into this young boy's body." Ragnar gestured to Max, who gave a little wave to the audience. "So now he has the ability to manipulate fire and lava and is joining the fight against the Ne'faro."

The elders cheered. "And speaking of the Ne'faro," Ragnar continued, "we need to sign a treaty that says Ignis will help Earth and the other Elemental planets, and vice versa. All for it, raise your hands."

Every elder in the room raised their hand.

"And that's a unanimous vote. All right. I'll sign this paper." A paper appeared in front of Ragnar, and he signed it with a small weak flame.

"Done," Ragnar said. "All right. It's nice seeing my people again. But bye!" With that, the Ragnar clone disappeared with a puff of fire, sealing the deal. Max walked back out the door, grinning as Ragnar said, *You owe me one.*

* * * * *

Ashleigh raced through the electric atmosphere of Zulcae-15, electricity coursing through her veins. *This feels amazing!* she thought happily. The moment she entered the planet, she fell in love. There were electrical storms everywhere and no rain. Thunder boomed, and lightning sizzled. She landed her Starcycle, removed her helmet, and jumped off. *What have I been missing?* she thought.

She placed her feet on the sandy ground, enjoying the landscape. From where she was, she could see a city with lights, civilians strolling across the ground. There were large buildings made of fulgurite (though Ashleigh didn't know what on earth that was)—lightning struck sand that turned into silica glass. Glass on the inside and a sand cover on the outside. *It's beautiful,* Ashleigh thought.

Welcome to my home planet, Vira said happily.

All of a sudden, a figure appeared in front of Ashleigh. The figure had ghostly-white skin with raven-black hair that barely touched its ears. All its clothing was black. Its eyes were colorless. *And that's not creepy at all,* Ashleigh thought sarcastically.

"Hello. I have been expecting you," the figure said.

"Who, or rather *what*, are you?" Ashleigh asked tentatively.

"Where are my manners? I am Void," the figure replied. "The higher-ups told me to kill you, and they'd give me a large sum of money. 'Void, you are to kill that female nuisance for fifty thousand ne'ans! As the best male mercenary we have, we're trusting you to do your job!'"

"Oh, okay," Ashleigh said. "Whenever you want to go. Take your time."

Before Void could respond, Ashleigh activated her lightning cloak and shot forward, slamming her fist into Void's gut. Void was thrown backward into a rock several meters away, crumpling to the ground. *You are really good at that,* Vira noted.

Void got to his feet, shaking his head to clear his thoughts. Ashleigh jumped forward again, aiming a punch at Void's head. But when Ashleigh reached Void, her fist went straight through his forehead. "What?" Ashleigh yelled, pulling her fist out.

Void grabbed her arm, grinning. "Right. You didn't know I could do that." Void twisted Ashleigh's arm around her back, making her yelp in pain. Ashleigh kicked Void with her left foot, but he turned intangible, dodging the blow. But that also meant releasing Ashleigh from his grip. Ashleigh jumped back several feet, grinning to herself.

So you can't isolate your intangibility to a certain part of your body, huh? she thought.

Use that to your advantage, Vira said.

What else did you think I was going to do?

Vira was silent. Ashleigh shrugged, thinking, *Normal lightning moves at about 220,000 miles per hour. If I called down natural lightning, it'd hit the ground in about a hundredth of a second. That would probably be faster than Void could react. But first I'll need to distract him.*

Ashleigh created two lightning clones, sending them toward Void with lightning daggers and their lightning cloaks activated. They shot forward, engaging in hand-to-hand combat. Or more precisely, hand-to-*air* combat. Sixty percent of their attacks landed, but the 40 percent of the attacks that went through Void were only because he got lucky.

The Ashleighs slashed and cut at Void, though not blitzing him. With their immense speed, they could have, but that wasn't the plan. The real Ashleigh raised her hands, channeling all the lightning within an acre of her. Bright-white lightning flashed and arced above her in the clouds, loud thunder crashing only a couple seconds afterward. Ashleigh could feel the tiny hairs on her arms standing on end, positive charges filling them.

A half-acre-long ring formed in the sky, lightning swirling around in it. Ashleigh kept the lightning going, watching Void. Void had no clue what was going on in the sky but was instead focused on evading the Ashleigh clones. Ashleigh dropped her arms, and thunder clapped. Not a moment later, a giant spiraling bolt of lightning spun down from the lightning ring. Other bolts of lightning fed into it, increasing its size until it was nearly seven meters wide and half a mile high. Void didn't realize what was happening until it was too late.

The lightning struck the ground with a loud *BOOM!* rocking the ground and sending sand flying into the air. Ashleigh was thrown backward, and her clones were completely obliterated. The brightness and loudness of the lightning called the attention of citizens from the city, and they rushed toward the scene.

When the lightning disappeared, the scent of burning plastic wafted into Ashleigh nostrils, causing her to sneeze. She rubbed her eyes to get rid of the lingering spots, blinking a couple times to adjust. She stared at the space around where the lightning had hit, gasping in amazement. Sandy structures were raised above the ground in a spiral shape, three branches forming near the top of it. *That is what humans call fulgurite, or as we call it, petrified lightning,* Vira explained.

Void was nowhere to be seen, and Ashleigh assumed the worst. "That was awesome!" she muttered to herself. But then the inhabitants of the planet landed around her, surrounding Ashleigh. Lightning flashed as electricity swirled around their arms, ready to attack.

Vira!

They don't know you. Stay calm. Don't panic and don't attack. Create a clone and shape it like me. I'll do the talking for you.

Taking her partner's advice, Ashleigh created a clone beside her, shaping its features and increasing its height. Vira's dirty-blonde hair appeared, and her calm, collected expression formed on the clone's face. When Ashleigh was done, the Zulcaeans gasped.

"Hello, my fellow Zulcaeans," Vira greeted calmly.

"Aren't you supposed to be dead?" one of the older Zulcaeans asked.

"Yeah," Vira said. "But as a last act, I transferred my powers to this young girl, Ashleigh, and have inhabited her ever since. Anyway, we need to sign a treaty that says we'll help the other planets and Earth in fighting the Ne'faro, and vice versa. All against it, show your hands."

Four hands out of the nearly thousand people raised. Everyone glared at the four people, and they quickly dropped their hands. "Unanimous vote for it then," Vira said. A piece of paper formed in her hand, and she signed it with a weak spark of electricity. "And my work here is done," she said. "I'll see you guys some other time. Peace!" With that, Vira disappeared.

Thanks, Ashleigh said to Vira.

No problem. I'm good in that area.

With that, Ashleigh mounted her Starcycle, giving one last wave to the Zulcaeans.

* * * * *

Damian flew through the freezing environment of Glacies-9. Each breath turned into tiny icicles, dropping to the ground. *At least I'm immune to the cold*, he thought. Damian landed his Starcycle on the cold ice, taking in his surroundings. There were tall shiny ice buildings surrounding him, and civilians went about, minding their own business.

Then all of a sudden, Damian ducked. He didn't know why he did it or what he was ducking under, but he just did. A shiny ice arrow flew past his head, embedding itself in the ground. Damian turned around to face a girl that looked about eight years older than him, pressing a dagger to his throat.

146

"Umm, I didn't do anything wrong, did I?" Damian asked.

Get out of there, Crogan said.

Damian slid under the dagger, kicking the girl away. He created a sword and shield, preparing for battle. The girl grinned, nocking another arrow. She fired, and the arrow whistled through the air, aimed straight at Damian's head. But he brought his shield up, blocking the arrow with a satisfying *thwack!* The girl darted forward, engaging Damian with her dagger. Each time she swung, Damian either blocked it easily with his sword or used his shield. The girl quickly realized that she was getting nowhere. She jumped backward, and what seemed like a blizzard surrounded Damian, obstructing his view of the girl.

Don't let your guard down, Damian, Crogan said warily.

Damian raised his arms, and the blizzard died down. But when he looked for his assailant, she was nowhere to be seen. Then an arrow flew at his back. Damian reflexively blocked it with his shield, looking for the person who shot it. But when he looked behind him, he saw no one. Another arrow flew toward his neck, but Damian ducked under it, feeling the cold air coming from the arrow.

Damian created an ice dome around himself, realizing that he wouldn't need to rely on his reflexes if he was protected all round. A flurry of arrows peppered the dome, but none penetrated. The only impact they had were tiny cracks that filled themselves in automatically. But then the dome shattered, ice shards dropping to the ground. *Right*, Damian thought. *I'm fighting an ice user.*

The ice shards then vibrated, shooting up toward Damian. He blocked them with his shield, but then cold, icy chains shot out of the ground, keeping Damian's arms and legs locked in place. The girl then jumped out in front of Damian, black hair flying. Her dagger glinted from the light in the sky as it fell toward Damian's neck.

CHAPTER 17

Max Turns into a Phoenix

Ronan trudged through the tall, waving grasses of Venta-16. His cape billowed with the blustery winds.

I like this place, Wyat, he thought. *It really goes with my element. That's Venta-16 for ya.*

Ronan abruptly stopped moving, realizing that there was a cliff just a foot in front of him. But then, an arrow hit the ground right where he would have stepped had he kept moving. *What the—*

Another arrow flew at his face. Reflexively, he manipulated the air around him to push the arrow away.

Seems like someone's on to you, Wyat said. Another arrow blew past Ronan.

It's best I protect myself while trying to figure out where that came from, Ronan thought. With barely a movement, Ronan twisted the air around him into a swirling shield, pushing away anything within a six-meter radius of him. Now focused, Ronan scanned his surroundings. The grasses were waving normally in the wind, but Ronan couldn't see anything out of the ordinary. Then all of a sudden, a green four-legged creature erupted from the ground right in front of Ronan's feet. The creature was about seven feet in length with its tail and two feet high. Four red slits for eyes adorned its face, along with a mouth full of hundreds of tiny but razor-sharp teeth.

The creature lunged at Ronan, but he dodged it by a foot, jumping to the side. The creature shook its head, disappearing into the ground. *What was that?* Ronan asked Wyat.

An Earth lizard. The only way to defeat it is keeping it off the ground. As long as its body is on the ground, there's no stopping it. And also, whatever you do, don't attack it if it's on the ground. It'll get bigger with each attack.

Thanks, Ronan said.

Another arrow whizzed past him. Ronan outstretched his arms, letting the wind around him shape itself into what he needed. The wind began to swirl more furiously, pulling grass and dirt from the ground. Ronan's hair whipped every which way, carried with the intense force of the wind. Ronan raised his arms, and the wind stopped for a second. All was silent for ten heartbeats. Then the sound of wind howling filled the air. All the wind around Ronan was expelled from its space, shooting out in a wide circle. Anything in its path was destroyed—the grass, dirt, rock, everything. Bits of greens and soil sprayed everywhere around Ronan, whipped around like insignificant scraps.

When the wind died down, Ronan dropped his hands, breathing slowly. *That was a very powerful attack*, he thought.

Definitely. But you executed it perfectly. And now that everything's in the open, you can see all your surroundings, Wyat noted.

Ronan nodded, scanning the land. Sure enough, a tall figure stood about twenty meters away from him. The space around them was slightly warped, but the distortions faded away after a couple seconds. The figure wore a gray mask, covering their mouth and nose. Their hair was a dark shade of brown, and they wielded a gray bow and arrow. Next to them stood the Earth lizard, except it was about two times as big. It was now fourteen feet in length and four feet in height. It growled, glancing up at the six-foot-tall figure next to it.

How did the thing grow bigger! I didn't attack it! Ronan asked Wyat.

It must have been when you used your wind attack. Maybe it came out of the ground again and took the attack, Wyat suggested.

The figure pointed at Ronan, saying, "You seem to be a worthy opponent. It is for that reason that I have to use my full power." The voice was rough and deep, signaling to Ronan that it was a male. The space around the man distorted again, and his bow and arrow glowed blue. A blue aura surrounded the man, and he tilted his face up.

Oh no, he's going super saiyan, Ronan thought sarcastically.

What's super saiyan? Wyat asked.

A phrase my grandpa used to say before he died. I think it had something to do with an old TV show.

The aura pulsed outward, causing the dirt and grass to flow up again. Then it settled to the ground, revealing the man, except this time, glowing blue with the bow and arrow now more pointed at the ends, blue in color, and looking like ice. The man raised the bow, stringing three glowing arrows. He fired them at Ronan, his aim perfect despite how far away he was. But Ronan grinned, turning into wind and moving away at the last second.

But then the spaces beside the arrows distorted, and they changed direction as if bouncing off invisible walls in the air. They followed Ronan as he reappeared on the ground, making glowing trails in the air as they flew. *Seeker arrows, huh?* Ronan thought.

"I feel honored that you have to use seeker arrows to hit me," Ronan said.

"My pleasure! The arrows are extremely sharp, sharp enough to cut through even Earth lizards! But they won't kill you unless I want them to. Just try not to die from the explosions so I can have some fun," the man said, firing another three arrows.

Ronan ducked under the previous three, facing the new ones. *So they're also exploding arrows. Noted.*

Ronan raised his right index finger into the air, feeling the air currents. The three arrows behind him had just turned around, forming an equilateral triangle with the point facing the sky as they flew toward his back. The ones in front of him formed an equilateral triangle with the point facing the ground. As you've probably figured out, if Ronan simply ducked at the last moment, the arrows would just fly past one another. That meant that Ronan would need to alter the trajectory of the arrows.

With only about three seconds before the arrows hit him, Ronan raised his arms. *One.* He used the wind to pull the first arrow to the top. *Two.* The second arrow shifted a bit, matching up with the one behind Ronan. Everything was set. *Three.* It seemed like reality was crawling. The six arrows whizzed through the air, merely feet away from Ronan. Then the Earth lizard leapt out of the ground beside Ronan, snapping its jaws. On it rode the man, a glowing dagger in his hand. Ronan cleared his mind, focusing on the execution of his next move.

The arrows and dagger were only inches away from Ronan's chest, chin, and back, and the Earth lizard's teeth were merely three inches away from Ronan's face. Right as it seemed Ronan was about to die, Ronan turned into air, flying away from the arrows and Lizard. Right as he did so, the arrows sliced through the Earth lizard, piercing through its heart and killing it. But then the arrows slammed into one another with a loud crackling sound.

"No!" the man screamed.

The arrows disappeared with a bright-blue light, but then reappeared, flickering rapidly. An earsplitting explosion followed, and a powerful shock wave pulsed outward, burning anything in its way.

Ronan thanked his lucky stars that he wasn't in human form, or he would have been killed. The blast collapsed on itself before pushing outward once more. The entire field was burned, and smoke filled the air. Ronan turned back into a human, surveying what was once a grassy field. The ground was black, and there was no sign of the man or the Earth lizard. Ronan assumed the worst, shuddering.

The only thing unaffected in the space was his Starcycle. But aside from that, Ronan still had a job to do.

Ronan looked over the cliff beside him and scanned the city. From this high viewpoint, he could see buildings, figures, sculptures, and much more. The lights and technology looked great from up there, and it would probably look better at the bottom. Ronan then estimated the drop down. "Hmm," he muttered, "about 728 feet up."

On the count of three, Ronan told himself. *One, two, three!* He then proceeded to jump off the edge of the cliff. Ronan hurtled down toward the ground at breakneck speeds, the wind blowing his hair every which way. He folded his arms to his sides and kept his legs together—straight, to be exact. His speed increased even more. *This is fun!* he thought. *Why haven't I done this before?*

When Ronan landed on the surface of the city, he was wowed. The Ventas' innovative skills were more than awesome. He lifted himself a few feet off the ground and hovered through the city. Bright lights, cool technology—what wasn't to love about this place?

Ronan wandered around for a while, taking in the sights. It looked like a carbon copy of Earth, except this one had superpowered aliens. Wyat then buzzed in Ronan's head. *Create a wind clone that looks like me and have me do the talking. My people don't know who you are.* Ronan shrugged, doing as Wyat had asked. He created the clone of Wyat, imagining his features as he created it. Once he was done, he continued walking, this time with "Wyat" beside him.

Ronan had only walked ten meters when a group of Ventaeans swarmed him and Wyat.

"Wyat!" they cried. "We thought you were dead!"

"I was," Wyat said. "And still am. But I managed to get myself inside this young boy beside me."

Ronan gave a tiny wave to the mob.

"Anyway," Wyat continued, "Earth and the rest of the planets are under attack by the Ne'faro, and in order to win, we need every helping hand we can get. Earth wants to be part of it, so are you with me?"

By now, the mob of about twenty people had turned to somewhere around two thousand. "Yes, we are!" the crowd screamed.

"Great!" Wyat said, producing a scroll of paper. A powerful wind tore across the paper, making a signature out of the paper. "All right, I need to go. Bye!" Wyatt disappeared with a gust of wind.

With that, Ronan turned into air, flying back to the cliff. He dropped to the ground, reverting to human form. He mounted his Starcycle and put his helmet on, taking to the air. The HUD in the helmet flickered to life and scanned his surroundings. Ronan tried communicating with Max, and static buzzed in his ear. But after a minute, Max's voice finally poked through. "Hey, what's up?" he asked.

Ronan responded, "Coming back from Venta-16. You?"

Max paused before answering, "Going back to our base. I'm gonna send out a signal to them, telling them to rendezvous at base."

Ronan clucked his approval and turned, heading back toward Earth. "So did you get an agreement?" he asked, voice hopeful.

"Yes, but there's a catch. If we turn on them for any reason, they will hit us with fire and fury, the likes of which the world has never seen," he answered. Ronan jumped for joy and shuddered at the same time. He couldn't imagine the land of the free turned into a desolate wasteland.

Without warning, Max's smart earbud began to chime. Sure enough, it was his mom calling. *Why would she be calling me now? And how do I have a connection here?* he wondered. "Mom?"

"Hey, honey, just want to tell you, I'm going on a girls' night out with my friends, so help yourself to some pizza. And you can cook something else if you don't want that tonight. Oh! Gotta go. Love you, bye!"

"Bye, Mom," Max said. Suddenly, his HUD started flashing! "Pizza will have to wait," he muttered. He clicked the screen, and it pulled up a picture of HoverTech Industries. There was smoke coming from the bottom of the building, and the upper and middle parts of the structure looked like they were about to collapse. "Ronan," Max called over the speaker, "would you allow me the honor of joining me on a rescue mission?"

Ronan laughed over the speaker. "Yes."

Max sped up his Starcycle and blew straight toward Earth. The shield deployed just as he entered the atmosphere. He dove straight down, then aligned the Starcycle, setting it to driving mode. The wheels popped out, and he landed on the road. He revved the engine and took off toward the building, sweat building on his face. If he and Ronan didn't make it on time…

He came down from the sky, skidding on the road but quickly aligning himself. Using the satellite feature, Max zoomed in on the building, sending the picture to Ronan. The building was coming up straight ahead. He entered the parking lot but didn't stop driving. "Let's give this thing called sticky mode a test run," Max said to himself. He tapped the screen and drove straight toward the side of the building. The mode activated, and he drove right up the building. But unbeknownst to Max, Ronan was not far behind.

A man fell out through the window, and Max raced to catch him. All of a sudden, Ronan shot past Max, going after the man. Another person, this time a woman, jumped out of another window, screaming as she fell. Max raced after her, outstretching his hand. But as luck would have it, he missed by a centimeter. *Darn it!*

Then pink blur came out of nowhere and caught the woman. "Need some help? I figured you wouldn't be able to keep things together. Literally," Trina's voice projected through the speaker.

"Touché," Max muttered. He raced back up the building to help Ronan. The top part of the building lit on fire, and he pushed the Starcycle even faster. You see, this was the tallest building in Manhattan; and if anybody was trapped in there, if they fell, it would mean instant death.

Above him, Ronan helped a woman out of a window, but she resisted and screamed, "My children are in there!"

Ronan reassured her, saying, "My friend is right below me and can get your kids. They'll be fine. Don't worry."

Sure enough, Max jumped off his Starcycle right as he got to the window, climbing in. There were four small kids trapped between a wall and a fire. The flames licked at their feet, and they shrieked and cried. But one of the kids, presumably the oldest sister, jumped in front of her siblings to protect them, bravely staring down the fire. *She's really brave and selfless to do something like that,* Max thought. He sprinted toward them, running straight through the fires. He picked them up and, with one last burst of adrenaline, jumped through the window.

The woman Ronan had helped out saw her kids, and tears welled in her eyes. Max nodded at Ronan, and he drove down the building with the kids' mother. "Hold on tight!" Max instructed the kids as he mounted his Starcycle, revving the engine. They held on to one another, and Max drove, descending the building. They reached the bottom of the building, and Max set the kids down on the ground with their mother. But then several pieces of debris fell from the top of the building, heading for a group of police and firefighters and the woman and her kids.

"Ronan!" Max called. "Double time!"

Ronan nodded and removed his helmet, running at superspeed to move all the rescue teams out of the way. Trina jumped in the way just as the debris neared the ground, unsheathing her sword and slicing the debris piece. She levitated the smaller pieces away from anybody that could be harmed, saving the family.

"Trina! Boost me!" Max yelled, an idea blooming in his brain.

Trina gave Max a burst of telekinesis, shooting him straight to the top of the building. Fire raged around him, but he was unfazed. He stepped into the flames and closed his eyes, drawing all the fire in the building to him. He raised his arms, and the fire followed, moving into the air. The fire swirled around him, and other flames in the room joined the human solar system.

A fiery bird shape formed around Max, and all heat in the room was solely produced from him. Max opened his eyes, enjoying the feeling of the fire. He climbed out of the window, hovering in the air. He spread his wings as far as they could go, blocking out the sun. *I feel so free!* he thought.

Ragnar made a chuckling sound in Max's mind, agreeing with him. People covered their eyes, wondering just what this thing was. At the moment, Max was the center of the world! Or something. Using the psychic link, Max called Trina and Ronan, and they flew off into the sky: one phoenix and two Starcycles.

CHAPTER 18

Beware the Mutant Caterpillars!

They flew on into the Panther constellation and split up to get the remaining team members. Ronan flew to Oceanum-22 while Trina went to Glacies-9. Max flapped his wings faster and entered the atmosphere of Zulcae-15.

Only one word can describe the experience of Zulcae-15: electrifying. Only someone like Ashleigh could survive this. Even in phoenix form, Max could barely survive. A bolt of lightning struck his right wing, and he screeched loudly, spiraling down toward the ground. His form flickered, and for a split second, he looked just like himself, but then turned back into a phoenix.

Max tried to stabilize himself, but his right wing was paralyzed. Shrieking, he breathed a ball of flame, hoping someone would see it. Luckily, he had good karma at the moment, and it decided to let him off the hook. Lightning swirled and flashed around him and slowed his fall. It created something like a tornado and set him down gently on the ground. Ashleigh stood there smirking as Max's phoenix form faded and his vision blurred. "Hey, I'm the tornado guy," he said before passing out.

Doesn't Max know that this place is basically my home turf? And plus, why was he a phoenix? The world may never know. Ashleigh dragged Max to her Starcycle, setting him down gingerly on the seat and barely fitting herself in front of him. She put on her helmet and lifted off.

Ashleigh jetted into space, turning on her speaker with a crackling sound. "Where is everyone?" she asked.

Ronan responded, "I'm nearing Earth. Jessica's with me right now."

"I'm nearing Earth too. Ashleigh's with me," said a voice from behind Ashleigh.

Ashleigh turned around, and Max winked at her. Rolling her eyes, Ashleigh said, "You couldn't hear him, but Max said we're nearing Earth as well. Meet you at base."

Then a weird tingly feeling entered Ashleigh's arms, almost as if she was about to be struck by lightning or something. Not that it would hurt her, though. All of a sudden, WHACK! Another vehicle sent them flying! Ashleigh floated decameters away, thinking, *What was that? What was that?! What was that!* before stopping herself and looking for her ride. The Starcycle was only about thirty meters away and was fine. Max was already climbing onto the vehicle.

Ashleigh floated toward the Starcycle and mounted, looking around for the other vehicle. But then she spotted Ronan and Jessica mounting their Starcycles. Instantly, she put two and two together. Their flight paths had intersected, and they had collided.

Grinning, Ashleigh spoke over the speaker, "Don't worry. I have insurance." They all took a moment to burst out in laughing fits. When Ashleigh recovered, she revved the engine and resumed her course, this time with Ronan and Jessica in tow.

A couple minutes later, Ashleigh and the rest landed their Starcycles on the small platform of the building and slowly drove into the garage. The kids dismounted and removed their helmets. When Max pointed at Ashleigh's hair in confusion, Ashleigh groaned inwardly. The helmets did *not* prevent helmet hair. They definitely weren't supposed to become a brand-name product.

They quickly rushed up the stairs, going into their room. Inside, they found Trina lying on her bed and munching popcorn. "Hey, guys," she said through a mouthful of popcorn.

"Where," Ashleigh wondered, "did you even get that?"

She swallowed and answered, "Turns out that I can make things appear from stores and movie theaters too. Grabbed this one out of a portal to Craig's Movie and Cinema."

Ashleigh's jaw on the floor quickly lifted into an evil grin, which everyone else in the room shared. "I wonder," she asked innocently, "if you can get me a root beer."

Trina groaned.

Soon after, everyone was sitting on their bed, either sipping drinks or munching snacks. Ashleigh chewed a doughnut and sipped her root beer. "I never realized just how hungry or thirsty I was until now," she said.

Then Damian and Connor barged into the room, their hair in disarray. They both collapsed on their beds, chests heaving. Damian wheezed, "Someone get me a Mountain Dew," before fainting on the spot.

Connor sat up. "I too would like this Mountain Dew."

Trina huffed and produced two Mountain Dews. Connor took one. Damian spontaneously shot up and grabbed the second one. They both drank with contented sighs.

Max asked, "Are you two even supposed to have caffeine?"

"First of all, it's caffeine-free Diet Mountain Dew. Second of all, you're one to talk, considering the Pepsi you just sipped," Damian shot back.

Max gave him an icy glare and sipped again.

Jessica piped up. "All right, you two, spill it. What happened?"

Damian shared a glance with Connor, and he responded with a nod. They spoke simultaneously, flapping their arms. "Four words: *beware the mutant caterpillars!*"

Max snorted Pepsi out of his nose, and Ashleigh choked on her doughnut. "W-what!" she choked out in between a laughing outburst. She wiped tears of laughter from her eyes.

"But it's true!" Damian whined. "We actually fought giant razor-jawed caterpillars just off the inner Kuiper Belt."

"Sounds realistic enough." Trina shrugged, stifling a laugh.

Then an alarm blared, interrupting their social time. "Great. More trouble." Ashleigh sighed. "What did *I* do to you, world?"

The kids set their snacks down, rushed into the elevator, and set the course for the main room.

They emptied out of the elevator and came in to a scene of discord. About several dozen masked bandits were under laser fire from the defense mechanisms in the room while others were trying to pry out the kids' tech. Max tightened his fists. "Can't we just eat in peace!"

Trina stepped forward, creating two double-ended scythes in her hands. She began to twirl them around, grinning. "May I?" she asked, focused on the bandits.

"Permission granted," Max said.

Instantaneously, Trina shot forward, spinning her blades. Any bandit in her way was either maimed or halved. Nothing more, nothing less. The rest of the kids followed her lead, disposing of any bandit left from Trina's attack.

The beautiful glowing scythes moved in tandem. *Spin, slice. Spin, slice.* The bandits didn't stand a chance. Sure, they were armed with laser rifles, but Trina didn't let them use them. *They're only tools if you use them. If you don't get a chance to use them, why bother?* Trina sliced through a shoulder, impaling another in the stomach. Then she dropped her scythes, punching the last one in the face. The bandit flew halfway across the room, skidding on the floor.

Trina then opened several portals under the bandits, sending them dropping somewhere in the Atlantic for sharks to feed on. She yawned, turning around.

"Those thugs interrupted a perfectly good snack. That, and they were way too easy to beat," Trina said. "Now who's up to finishing it?" She teleported away, and Max followed her, pyro-porting into the room. Ashleigh used the stairs, and everyone else followed her lead because *they* weren't showoffs.

Anyway, in the room, Ashleigh finished her doughnut and washed it down with her root beer. Again someone seriously needed to find out why root beer tasted like toothpaste! This was a serious crisis. Ashleigh chucked her can into the trash and sighed contently. Then a dark thought hit her. "Has anyone seen Emily?"

Max looked at her, chewing a brownie. "She's probably just in the training room fighting the robots that the archers set up there," he said.

Trina looked up from her popcorn, saying, "Lemme check."

After about two seconds, she said, "Max is right. She is."

"Did you even look?" Ashleigh asked.

"Mm-hmm."

"No, you didn't."

"Your loss."

With a flick of her wrist, Trina teleported all of them to the training room.

When they reappeared, sure enough, there was Emily, fighting off a dozen training robots.

"Told you!" Trina said.

Emily turned around, unleashing a powerful gravity wave on the robots surrounding her. "What did you guys need?"

"Well, first," Trina said, producing another bag of popcorn, "are you hungry?"

Emily outstretched her arm, pulling the bag of popcorn out of Trina's hands with gravity. "I've been fighting off robots, and you *ask* me if I'm hungry?"

Ashleigh grinned. "See! Told you guys I liked her."

"*Second*," Trina started, glaring at Ashleigh, "you up for an obstacle course?"

Emily opened her mouth, levitating and eating popcorn exponentially quicker than physically possible. When finished, she said, "Yep. When are you starting?"

They all lined up at the leftmost end of the room and prepared to start. "The rules!" Damian called. "You can use your powers and team up with one another temporarily. No tripping, though. That's off-limits. If you are caught tripping people, you will be taken out of the game. And Trina and Max may not teleport. Duplicate Trina will announce when to begin."

The duplicate appeared in front of them. "On your marks!" she called. "Get set, GO!" The kids took off on the obstacle course. The first ten meters were easy; they were just running forward. After that, things became harder. Just as Emily neared the first obstacle, a pit opened under her feet. She fell in but grabbed the ledge. She then pushed herself up by negating the gravity around her.

From that moment forward, Emily decided to fly the rest of the course. She heard the whizzing of an object behind her and flew higher to dodge it. An electric javelin pierced through where her head would have been only two seconds before. She threw a ball of compressed gravity at Ashleigh in retaliation. She dodged it with relative ease—hand springing over it. She flew over the first obstacle, a giant wall. Then just a couple meters after, she almost met certain doom in the form of a barrage of flying boulders.

Weaving in between the boulders, Emily decided that the air was too dangerous and joined everyone else down on the ground. Ashleigh, Trina, Ronan, and Emily were in the lead, with Max and Jessica in second, and Damian and Connor in third. Ashleigh threw a bolt of lightning across toward Ronan, and he disappeared into thin air. He reappeared behind Ashleigh and kicked her from the back.

Ashleigh fell onto the ground but picked herself back up quickly. This time, she had a score to settle. She rapid-fired lightning javelins at Ronan, and several of them hit their target. Ronan went down in a cry of fury. Trina sent a wave of energy at Ashleigh, and she tripped over Ronan. Then Emily negated the gravity around Trina, and she went floating into the air. But Trina snapped her fingers, and the gravity negation stopped, allowing her to hover in front of Emily.

She aimed a kick at Emily's stomach, but Emily created a pressure barrier and blocked it. Emily then threw several gravity spheres at Trina, and they all made the mark. Emily was finally in the lead. She jumped over spikes on the ground, dodged flying boulders, and jumped across land mines for what seemed like an eternity. That is, until her legs attached themselves to the ground.

It seemed that her feet had become one with the ground. She literally couldn't move at all. A blast of ice ensured that she wouldn't be mobile any time soon. She saw the rest of the kids closing in on her. But Emily had an ace up her sleeve. As they neared her, Emily charged her energy, shooting it outward. The gravity pulse threw everyone backward, and her feet came free.

Grinning, Emily gave the flag at the end of the course its own gravity, and it pulled her toward it, pulling her faster than everyone else to the finish line. She was almost there! She gave one last push as Damian shot a blast of ice at her leg. Jessica's water powered it, and it flew faster and faster. Emily rolled past the finish line and took away the gravity from the flag when she grabbed it. "Yes!" she screamed in victory. She was victorious!

CHAPTER 19

Becoming a Cat Burglar Is a Very Healthy Lifestyle Choice— You Should Try It Sometime!

"Nice job, Emily!" Max said cheerfully, grinning at Emily.

"Thanks," Emily said happily while Trina poured confetti over her head. "But now that, that's over, we're gonna need some new recruits. Right?"

"Right," a voice said from behind the kids. Quicker than any regular human could react, Ashleigh created her lightning dagger, turning around and pointing it in the direction the voice came from.

"Chill out!" the voice said. "And by the way, I'm on the ground."

The kids all looked at the ground, and sure enough, a shadow looked up at them, grinning. Ashleigh threw her lightning dagger at the shadow, but it spread out of the way, twisting itself up out of the ground. It then formed a human figure with raven-black hair just like Damian's, and brown eyes. Its hair was gelled and spiky and silver at the tips. Its jeans were black and ripped on its left knee, and they wore red sneakers.

"Wait a minute," Damian said, narrowing his eyes. "That's Jake!"

Damian grinned, high-fiving Jake. "How are you doing, cousin?"

"Cousin!" the others exclaimed. "He's your cousin?"

"Yep," Damian said. "We're cousins. Although *I'm* older than him by four months."

Jake rolled his eyes. "Anyway, you said you needed new recruits, so here I am!"

"So what's your power exactly?" Max asked.

"Shadows. I can control darkness, shadows, that stuff. I can also turn into a shadow, as you saw earlier," Jake replied.

"Great!" Max said. "You'd be useful for stealth missions!"

Jake's face darkened. "*Stealth missions?* Is that the only thing you think I'm useful for?"

Jake clenched his fist, and Max's shadow snaked around him, binding him. Jake's shadow then turned into a silhouette of him, pitch-black. It walked to Max, creating a black staff in its hands. "So you said I was good for stealth missions, right?"

"Uhh, never mind," Max said, straining his voice.

"Great!" Jake said happily, releasing Max.

All of a sudden, the alarm went off. The giant screen on the control panel flashed white and blue. Max's shadow enlarged and hardened into a double-ended scythe, and Jake grabbed it. "What's going on?" he asked, eyebrows furrowed.

Max sprinted to the screen, and he reached for the control pad. A picture of Luke's Jewelry & Fashion Mall appeared on screen. "Give me a report," Max commanded, and a holographic businessman appeared on screen.

It said, "A cat burglar robbed the Luke's Jewelry & Fashion Mall downtown last night. That is the most expensive and most prestigious company in the US. Every piece of jewelry is guarded by randomly moving lasers. The entire place is covered in lasers after hours. The cat burglar would need to be highly agile and flexible to get past that type of security. They haven't captured a picture of the burglar, but from evidence they've captured, police say they're expecting them again tonight. That's now. My camera just spotted the burglar on the move to the mall. You need to cut them off before they get there."

Trina got up, and her sword appeared in her hand. "Well, guess we better get going."

They donned their suits, and Trina created new ones for Jake and Emily. Jake's was a smooth leathery black with a flowing black cape. Emily's was a pearl-gray color and had a glittering cape. The kids rushed down the stairs, entering the garage. Trina duplicated the Starcycles and helmets, adding two more for Jake and Emily.

"If you've ridden a bicycle before, it's just like this. Except bicycles can't hover, and they aren't motorized," Trina explained.

They mounted their Starcycles, pulling on their helmets, and they then rode into the night. They weaved through the traffic and set their GPSes to go to Luke's Jewelry & Fashion Mall.

Trina spoke over the speaker, "Emily, Jake, we officially welcome to the team. Hope you enjoy the rush 'cause there's gonna be a lot of it."

"I love the streets even more when it's dark, and dark it is. You can see all the lights better, and there's just such a pretty contrast," Jessica said. They continued to drive, slipping in the gaps between cars.

After a couple minutes, they reached the entrance to the mall and parked their bikes. Removing her helmet, Trina noticed a black hovercycle parked nearby and turned to the doors. She opened a portal, gesturing for them to get in. "C'mon!" she urged. "Time's a wastin'!"

Emily, Ashleigh, Jessica, Damian, Ronan, and Trina stepped in and appeared on the other side of the doors. Max, Connor, and Jake appeared next to them.

Lasers covered the entire space from top to bottom. There was practically no room to move. For regular humans, anyway. Jake turned into a shadow and moved silently across the floor. In his shadow form, he was not only flat but also invisible in the darkness. The only time he was visible was when he slid under a laser. Max pyro-ported to the other end of the room and waved at the others cheerily. Connor disappeared under the floor and reappeared next to Max. Ronan turned into a gust of wind and blew across the room, appearing next to Connor.

Trina opened another portal, and everybody else stepped inside. They reappeared on the other side with the boys. They then dashed into the jewelry room and met even more lasers. But this time, they were moving across the room, covering every space at least once. From the window, the kids could see the moon pouring white eerie light into the room. Suddenly a triangle of glass opened from the window, and in came a woman dressed in a tight black leather suit. She wore black heeled boots with leather gloves.

"What are you kids doing here?" she hissed from the window. She crouched and leaped, flipping in the air and landing in a crouch right on top of a glass case.

"I could ask you the same thing," Max replied, thinking, *This woman takes the term "cat burglar" to the next level.*

The woman raised one hand, saying, "Guess you'll have to catch me to find out." She leapt on top of the stairs and jumped back onto the window ledge. She sat down and kicked her legs back and forth. Trina teleported next to her on the ledge, but the woman slashed at her with an electric baton she'd produced from her suit. Trina blocked the hit with a shield, kicking the woman off the window.

But the lady landed on a glass cover, leaping across the room and jumping onto the stairwell parallel to the one the kids were on. She waved to the rest of the crew mockingly. Jake turned into a shadow and slid across the floor, appearing next to her. He turned her shadow into a staff and cornered her onto the wall. "Time's up," he said.

"Before I go, I have something to say," the woman pleaded.

Jake cocked his head. "What?"

"Becoming a cat burglar is a very healthy lifestyle choice—you should try it sometime!" the lady said.

She then kicked Jake in the stomach, slipping away. She bounded off the wall and jumped off Max's head as she made her way to the stairs where Trina now stood. Max took off after her, leaping across the cases. But then the burglar grabbed a case and threw it at Max, saying, "Catch!"

Max instinctively dived for the case, not wanting such precious material to be broken. But that was all part of the plan. The cat burglar pulled out a small laser pointer from her pocket, clicking a button. She focused it on a glass case holding a diamond necklace worth $578, 346.

The red laser sliced through the glass, and the burglar made a circle big enough for her hand to fit in. She tucked the laser away, pulling out the diamond necklace. *This will definitely help my mas-*

ter pay for his project, she thought. She then pocketed the necklace, climbing on top of the glass. "See you kids later!" she said, leaping about forty feet to the window. She then threw her electric baton at Max before jumping out. The baton spun in the air, moving straight toward Max. He was unaware, solely focused on balancing the case and standing on one at the same time. The baton hit his leg, and Max tripped, falling. He hit the ground, thinking that he'd missed a laser. But oh, how wrong he was.

The alarms blared, and lights flashed in the room. "Crud, crud, crud—*into the portal*." Trina screamed, opening a portal on the ground. They rushed in, barely escaping the police officers that filed into the room at that moment. The kids reappeared outside, where police vehicles and officers waited, laser rifles pointed at them.

"Hands up!" one shouted, and the kids did as they said. But then Jessica created a thick fog, rushing the kids to their Starcycles.

The cat burglar mounted her bike behind the police officers' backs. She winked at the kids and strapped her helmet on, pulling out of the parking lot. The kids followed suit, shooting after her. Trina turned on the radar on her Starcycle and scanned the area. The cat burglar was already driving down the street. "She's getting away!" Trina screeched over the speakers. "Turn your lights on and follow me," Trina ordered, rounding the corner.

CHAPTER 20

GPSes Are Awesome, No Exceptions

The burglar was right in front of Trina, practically close enough that she could touch her if she tried. Trina tapped her Starcycle's screen, activating autopilot. She needed to do *something.* Anything. Scanning the burglar's hovercycle, Trina's helmet's HUD pulled up the components of the vehicle. *Huh,* Trina thought, *didn't know it could do that.*

Trina clicked the right side of her helmet, linking it to the computer in the main room. "Which of these parts would be best to target?"

"My system says the two hover motors that allow for flight on the hovercycle. That and the OverDrive reactor. That would make it impossible for the hovercycle to take to the air or blast off faster than you could imagine," said the computer voice.

"Okay," Trina said, grinning and swiping her screen to look for her missiles. There were heat-seeking missiles, Starcycle-controlled missiles, laser missiles, and much, much more. But what Trina really needed was tiny, almost-microscopic missiles that would travel into the hovercycle and take it out from the inside. And if needed, track it until they are set to explode. Luckily, the Starcycle had just what she needed. "Tiny exploding trackers," the Starcycle screen called it.

Then a thought hit Trina. *What exactly is she going to be doing with that $578, 346 necklace? And how exactly is she able to jump so far? No regular human can do that. And where is she going with that? Better find out with these.* Trina tapped the screen several times, releasing the trackers. Ten of them flew in through a tiny crack in the fuel door, making their way into the hover motors and OverDrive reactor. Only one latched onto the cat burglar's clothes, ensuring that if she left the hovercycle, she'd still be tracked. Trina then released a small regular tracker that attached itself to the front of the hovercycle.

The kids then continued their chase, evading other cars and vehicles on the road. The burglar glanced at her mirrors, watching the kids getting closer. *Can't be caught now*, she thought. *I need to put up a distraction.* She clicked a button on her hovercycle, and it released a black thick smoke that covered the entire road, blocking their views of the burglar and obscuring regular vision for any drivers.

Ronan acted quickly, using a gust of wind to clear out the smoke, but by the time he did, the burglar was gone. "Oh, come on! We go to all that trouble just to lose her?" Ronan yelled exasperatedly.

Trina snorted. "You think we lost her? Let's get back to base, and I'll show you something." She created a six-foot-tall portal in front of them, gesturing to them to follow her as she drove in.

When they reappeared in the garage, Max and the rest dismounted and removed their bikes, shouting, "We can't let her get away!"

"Yeesh, guys!" Trina yelled back. "I'm not dense. I know that. That's why I planted several exploding tracking devices in her hovercycle."

The others recoiled in shock.

"You did?" Max asked quietly.

"Yes," Trina said. "I just had to see where she was going with the necklace and what she was going to do with it. So I planted ten near-microscopic exploding trackers in the hover reactors allowing flight in the hovercycle. Now I just need to pull up the GPS on the big screen, if you'll allow me."

With that, Trina teleported to the main room, letting the others take the elevator. With the click of a button, Trina powered the computer on, letting it hum as its dark screen lit up. "Connect to my Starcycle GPS," Trina commanded.

The screen scanned her face, taking the data and connecting it to the Starcycle. After only a couple seconds, it pulled up the GPS, showing exactly where the trackers were. The screen was split: one-half showing the burglar's vehicle relative to space itself and the other one showing the immediate surroundings of the hovercycle. The others walked out of the elevator, moving to where Trina was.

"The GPS says the burglar is about half the distance to any of the Elemental planets. She could be going to any of them, so we need to wait and watch. But in the meantime, I'm going to upload the tracking system to your GPSes," Trina said.

She swiped the control pad, clicking a few buttons. "The computer's going to need to scan your faces. Get in the group."

Everyone except Trina moved directly in front of the screen, letting it scan them. After about a minute, the GPS system was uploaded, now on the other Starcycles. And the burglar was nearing Naturae-37. But then the burglar took a sudden turn, aiming for a blue-and-brown planet right next to Naturae.

"Anybody here know what that planet is called?" Trina asked, confused.

Everybody turned to Connor as he had the most knowledge of those planets among all of them. "Hmm," he vocalized, "I've seen it before, but I just can't remember the name."

Trina watched as the vehicle entered the planet, the GPS becoming more focused on details and such. "GPSes are awesome, no exceptions. They let you track people, vehicles, tell you where to go so you don't need to waste brain power, etc. They're awesome," Trina said to herself, watching the screen. The hovercycle landed on the ground, its smooth crystal-covered tires rolling on the planet's road. "That's our cue, kids," Trina said, pointing at the hovercycle. "That's where we need to go."

About five minutes later, the kids were driving across the ground, making rapid progress in their chase of the burglar. According to the GPS, the burglar was less than a mile away, which was a length the kids could cover in less than a minute.

"Get ready," Trina said.

Then Connor said, "I now remember what the name of this planet is! It's Ne'far, the home planet of the Ne'faro."

That got the others' attention. "So what you're saying is we're on enemy turf right now," Max said.

"Yep," Connor agreed.

"Then we have to tread lightly. We don't want to attract unwanted attention," Trina said.

Then their GPSes began to beep, signaling to them that they had reached their destination. They parked their Starcycles and removed their helmets. A tall glass building stood in front of them, almost a thousand meters high and majestic.

"Is this the place?" Jake asked.

"Looks like," Trina said, spotting the burglar's hovercycle nearby. Just then, Trina felt something in her pocket. Reaching in, she pulled two small disks from her pocket, each about one centimeter in diameter. Realizing their use, she placed both on them in her eyes, like contacts, blinking a few times to get used to the feeling. When she opened her eyes, an HUD like the one in her helmet appeared, GPS and all, in the contacts. *Thank you, archers*, Trina thought to herself. She scanned her surroundings, activating the GPS tracking system.

The GPS came on, showing the exact location of the cat burglar. She was inside the building, already sprinting up the stairs to the top. "There!" Trina said, pointing to the black silhouette.

Jake wasted no time, turning into a black shadow falcon and scaling the building. The others followed suit, flying up the building after Jake. Jake flapped his wings, speeding up. The burglar was only a few more stories above him, but she was moving faster than he would have assumed. *Five stories…four stories…three stories…two stories…one story.*

Turning back into a human, Jake glanced at a shadow behind the cat burglar, teleporting into it. *Shadow teleportation is so convenient in times like these*, he thought. He quickly switched into shadow form, merging with the cat burglar's shadow. He followed her as she dashed up the stairs, smoothly slipping across the steps. The cat burglar finally stopped in front of a door, reaching out to open it. But right before she touched it, Jake made a sign with his hands, and the shadows around him turned into tendrils, wrapping around the burglar.

Right after that, the rest of the team appeared next to him, weapons at the ready. The burglar's eyes narrowed, and the shadow tendrils shot off her, tearing and slamming into the ground. She sprang to her feet, flipping onto the wall in a crouch. She pulled out two electric batons, enlarging them into staves.

The woman then sprang at the kids, swinging her staves. But before she could hit anyone, Emily pushed her back with a burst of gravity. The burglar landed on the ground, dropping her electric staves. "I see a direct approach won't work on you," she said, pulling out six exploding disks from her pockets.

The burglar threw the disks in a wide arc, picking up one of her staves. She smashed the window with it, jumping out with a wink. Emily reacted quickly, making a distorted gravity field around them. The exploding disks slowed as they entered the field, moving as if in slow motion. Emily and the others quickly moved out of the space, following the burglar out of the window.

Damian shot down the building, sending a beam of ice at the burglar. It slammed into her legs, freezing them and increasing her falling speed. But then the woman outstretched her arms beside her, and black leather gliding wings stretched between her arms and her sides. Trina created a portal below her, dropping into it and reappearing next to the burglar. She created a glowing chain, wrapping it around her.

The cat burglar banked, trying to pull Trina along, but the extra weight was too much for the gliders to handle, and they plummeted toward the ground. Trina grabbed the cat burglar, flying the two of them toward the Starcycles. The others followed her lead. Trina flew down to her Starcycle, setting the burglar down behind her. She fastened the chain to the Starcycle, ensuring that the burglar couldn't escape.

Trina then levitated the diamond necklace out of the burglar's pocket, wrapping it around her wrist. The others mounted their bikes, following Trina as she opened a portal back to Earth.

About an hour later, the kids had turned the burglar in to the police, cleared everything up, and were back at their base, lying on their beds. It was 12:37 a.m., a little after midnight. Damian, Jessica,

Max, Ronan, Ashleigh, Emily, Jake, and Connor were asleep while Trina was just lying down, eyes open. Her mind was still racing, all thoughts on the Ne'faro. *Ne'far is the home of the Ne'faro*, she thought. *So if we eliminate Ne'far, take it out from the source, problem solved, right?* But her conscience thought otherwise. *Not all the Ne'faro are evil. Some of them are just little kids who don't know a thing about the war. Would I do the same if it were humans?*

After a little while, Trina's mental argument fizzled out, and she fell asleep, her mind finally at rest.

Nine hours later, Trina was up preparing breakfast. This time, it was waffles, syrup, and corn on the cob. Trina poured some waffle batter into the waffle maker, closed it, and let it cook. She then glanced at the cooling corn, about thirty ears of corn in a bowl, steam floating off it. The fragrant smell of waffles wafted into Trina's nostrils, and she opened the waffle maker, levitating the waffle onto a plate with ten waffles already stacked.

About a minute later, the others walked down the stairs, rubbing their eyes and yawning. "Hey, guys!" Trina said enthusiastically, levitating another waffle. "Breakfast is ready."

The kids sat down, each receiving a plate with a waffle and an ear of corn. After serving everyone, Trina sat down with a plate of her own, digging into the waffle while the corn cooled. "So what's next?" Ashleigh asked, taking a bite of her waffle.

Max swallowed a mouthful of corn, saying, "I'm not sure. Half of me thinks we should lie low for now, still working to get information about the Ne'faro and the war, but the other half of me thinks that's not enough. That we should be doing more."

"We need to train, first and foremost," Emily said. "We need to get better with our powers if we're to make an impact. We're playing a game of life and death, and in order not to die, we need to be at our best all the time. Not just when we feel like it. *All* the time."

"I agree with Emily," Trina said. "We need to improve. We have no idea what kind of enemies lie ahead, so we need to be ready. But, Max"—Trina took a bite of her waffle—"what do you think of an infiltration mission?"

About the Author

Jeffrey is a Duke University's 2018 PSAT 8/9 honoree and medal recipient for high achievement in reading and writing. Also a 2019 graduate of the University of Nebraska's Priceless Preteen Leadership Program, Jeffrey is inspired to promote diversity and empower people through his writings. He is an avid reader and owes his love of reading and writing to the Dolly Parton's Imagination Library through which he got one book every month until age six. Jeffrey's style of writing has been described as "one where you'll be right in the moment with the characters." Visit him at www.heisjeffrey.com.